MERMAID OF ST. MORITZ

MERMAID OF VENICE: BOOK FIVE

JINCEY LUMPKIN

ABOUT THE AUTHOR

JINCEY LUMPKIN is a writer who splits her time between NYC and Lisbon. She has been profiled by Dateline NBC, *Vice*, and *GQ*, among others. *Out* Magazine listed her in its "OUT 100", naming her as one of the world's most influential LGBTQ+ people, alongside celebrities like Laverne Cox and Ricky Martin.

Scan the QR code below to join my email newsletter or visit JinceyLumpkin.com/Front-Matter

facebook.com/jinceylumpkin

twitter.com/jinceylumpkin

instagram.com/storiesbyjincey

To request permissions, contact the publisher at jincey@jinceylumpkin.com

Ebook: 978-1-7376155-2-1
Print: 978-1-958452-99-8
Hardcover: 978-1-7376155-9-0

CIP Block/Library of Congress Number:
1-11485589381

First edition July 2022.

Edited by Amanda E. Clark
Cover art by Jason Brooks
Cover art direction by Matthew Axe
Cover layout by Lauren Balistreri & Ash Cheshire

To my Padinas, Robbi and Cat.

May we always have a garden with a big shade tree.

ACKNOWLEDGMENTS

As I continue my author journey, I deepen my understanding both of writing as a craft and of marketing. I want to thank my friends from Clubhouse for their many hours of support and encouragement.

Dear readers, I am sending you all my love. I adore reading your reviews (even the mixed ones!), and I look forward to emailing with you and talking on social media. It's always so fun to see the Easter eggs and bits of dialogue you pick up on.

A big thank you to my editor, Amanda, for her hard work. You keep me on track, and I love you for it!

Many, many thanks to Matthew Axe, Jason Brooks, Lauren Balistreri, and Ash Cheshire for bringing the book covers to life and making them so stunning.

Big kiss to my beautiful wife, Eva. These are trying times, and I thank you for always standing by me and supporting me.

I write this acknowledgment as I watch from afar as things fall apart in America. My home country is breaking my heart and wrecking the lives of so many. It is my sincere hope that we regain the progress for which we fought so fiercely. Maybe one day we will return to making progress and realize a more equal nation.

CONTENT ADVISORY

This book contains intense descriptions of graphic sex, violence, and abuse, including emotional abuse, murder, and torture.

MERMAID OF ST. MORITZ

1

April 5th

At the Parisian hideaway Florent had secured for Gia, Riley was snuggled into bed with Gia.

"I've been thinking," Riley whispered. "I want Florent to be our first."

Gia offered a sarcastic laugh. "Florent has no interest in a *ménage à trois*. I assure you that. He is annoyingly possessive."

"I'm not talking about *fucking* him! Oh, Jesus, is that what you thought?" Riley laughed. "Banish the thought!"

"Then what are you talking about?" Gia asked.

"I meant what I said in New York. I want to watch you kill someone. I think about it all the time. I want to be there with you. I want to help you. Let's kill Florent. Let's do it together. *Please*? It would be so much fun."

"*Assolutamente no!*" Gia insisted with finality. "Are you crazy?"

Riley furrowed her brow, obviously not following. "I'm confused. Isn't killing men your favorite thing to do? Sex-murder is basically sixty percent of your personality."

"You have no idea what you are on about," Gia snapped. "Have I killed before? Yes. But it is not so simple, Riley. My moves are always carefully planned. The eyes of the world are on me now, and I cannot afford to have a misstep. I must act with the utmost caution and stay under the radar."

But Riley pressed on. "I can be careful. Florent won't even see us coming for him."

"Florent is not an option."

Riley sat up, frustration written on her face. "What? Why? Are you in love with him or something? You told me you were scared of him... which is it?"

Gia blinked a few times, her mind sorting through confusing feelings.

Do I love Florent? Gia wondered. *How absurd, of course not. He is masochistic and controlling. But he does love me. Sometimes he disgusts me. Sometimes I crave him.*

Gia shrugged, deciding on an answer. "He knows too much about me."

But Riley wasn't placated by Gia's response. "So, wouldn't that give you even more reason to want to get rid of him?"

"I cannot *get rid of him*... I have certain constraints because of the contract I signed. The loan documents for the fifty million euros I borrowed from him contain an acceleration clause should anything happen to him."

"I don't speak legalese. What does that mean?"

Gia huffed in frustration. "Riley, if he dies, or I am arrested for any crime, the entire sum becomes due immediately."

"That's very inconvenient," Riley pouted. She gave herself a moment to think. "Then let's find someone else!"

"Murder is not a priority for me at the moment, Riley," Gia admitted.

"You're no fun."

Gia turned on her side to face Riley, hoping to achieve understanding between them.

"I have to focus on rebuilding my business portfolio. I want my life back. Can you not understand why I would want that?"

Riley reached out her hand and took Gia's chin into her palm. "Why don't we just see what happens, huh?"

2

April 5th

Harper watched in silence as her parents' ashes were lowered into their adjacent graves.

The Epstein-ing of the Langleys had made international news—it was a proper scandal—but Harper had found it odd that in the ten days that had followed her parents' untimely deaths, only one person had asked her about their funeral: Queen Mother Awa.

Flowers and fruit and baskets of every kind had arrived at the OTN office, at Langley Manor, and even at Harper's Manhattan apartment, and many people called or wrote with their condolences, but no one asked about the arrangements. Harper had not even considered the possibility that people would be relieved not to attend a joint funeral for her mother and father.

With no chorus line of elites ready to pay their respects, Harper decided that, post-autopsy, her parents would be cremated. Was that a particularly cruel way to handle their deaths? Absolutely, especially considering how upset Bronwyn had been over Harper's unilateral decision to cremate Cameron, resulting in what Bronwyn felt was not a traditional Christian burial.

Harper also opted not to have a priest oversee Royce and Bronwyn's burial. That part wasn't revenge, though. It was pure guilt.

Awa insisted on accompanying Harper to the family plot. There was no way she was going to let Harper deal with burying both her parents alone.

Once the cemetery's caretakers started shoveling dirt into the graves, Awa approached Harper and stroked her arm, whispering, "Why don't we go and let these men do what needs to be done?"

"I can't leave right now," Harper muttered through a clenched jaw. "I'll stay until it's over."

Awa lifted her hand to Harper's cheek and gently angled Harper's head toward her. "Child, it *is* over. Come with me and let's go have something good to eat."

* * *

BRONWYN'S German housekeeper served tea for Harper and Awa on the back porch. It was moderately cool outside, so Harper had switched on the heat lamps. The women watched as the setting sun spread a rose-gold blanket across the Hudson River Valley.

"Will you sell the house?" Awa asked quietly.

"No," Harper shook her head. "I can't, actually. It's held in trust. I suppose one day it will pass to Serena. I can't see myself ever having children."

Awa nodded, "I understand."

"Honestly, the thought of this huge house being empty creeps me out. The staff will still come to maintain the place, but it's just bizarre that Mom and Dad won't be here anymore."

"Maybe you can rent it out."

"I don't think I'm allowed to. But... why don't you ask Moussa and your wife to come and stay here for a while?"

"A kind offer, Harper, but we are in the midst of a war," Awa admitted.

"You can't have a fireside chat without a fire, can you? This place has about ten fireplaces. It could make a nice war headquarters for you."

"I would not want to overstay my welcome, dear."

"You wouldn't be," Harper said, leaning forward. "Sincerely, I am grateful to you for your support today and in the last few months. The network is doing better than ever... and that's largely thanks to you."

"I'll consider it," Awa replied.

In truth, Awa had already pictured herself running down to the bank of the Hudson for an early morning swim.

3

April 11th

Agents Clark and Sullivan observed Bryce Dean from behind a two-way mirror inside an interrogation room at FBI headquarters in Washington, D.C. He fidgeted in his seat as his attorney settled in the chair next to him.

Bryce's lawyer reached across the table and patted him on the hand. "Calm down, Mr. Dean. We will sort everything out."

After waiting a few moments to see if Bryce had revealed any incriminating information, the agents entered the room. Agent Clark held a thick folder, which she plunked down on the table as she took a seat.

"Good evening, Mr. Dean," Agent Clark said. "Can we get you anything? A water perhaps?"

"My client is fine," the lawyer answered. "If you don't mind, we would like to get an understanding of the charges. Mr. Dean has been in custody for over a week. When is his arraignment?"

"Oh, we have no plans to arraign Mr. Dean anytime soon."

"Excuse me?" the lawyer seethed. "Does the FBI not understand due process?"

"It's Mrs. Jones, right?" Agent Clark asked Bryce's attorney. "I think you'll find that judges tend to be much more lenient with the FBI when it comes to terrorists."

The lawyer's eyes widened at the accusation. "My client is not a *terrorist*."

Agent Clark opened her file, scanning its contents. "According to our investigation, Mr. Dean provided material assistance to his mother, *Queen* Karen Dean, when she attacked the nation of Senegal, killing hundreds of merfolk and four human citizens, as well as inflicting collateral damage along the coast of Dakar."

"Define his *alleged* material assistance," Jones demanded.

"Financial assistance, transportation, aiding and abetting a fugitive. From the evidence we have, this is a straightforward case of conspiracy to commit international terrorism."

Jones furrowed her brow. "I would like to see some of this *so-called* evidence."

Agent Sullivan smiled. "Perhaps that won't be necessary. We have a proposition for Mr. Dean. We would like to offer him immunity in exchange for his cooperation in bringing his mother to justice."

Jones glanced at Bryce, whose down-turned lips indicated his displeasure with the idea.

"Look at it this way," Agent Clark continued, "we would like to build a... *friendship*... with Mr. Dean."

Jones scoffed and rolled her eyes. "Sure, besties with the FBI. That seems reasonable."

"We've already established a very strong relationship with Queen Awa of Senegal," insisted Agent Clark. "But we would really love to get a window into the *other* side of this conflict. There's so much about the mermaid world that the American government doesn't understand. And, as you can imagine, we're keen to work with an American citizen. It's possible that our interests are more aligned than you might expect. Becoming a confidential informant for us would guarantee you not only blanket immunity but also... let's call it *special status* with the U.S. government."

There was a beat of silence before Bryce offered the subtlest bob of his head, showing his interest, if not his agreement.

"Write up your offer," Jones replied, "and we'll review it."

"You're a registered Republican, aren't you, Mr. Dean?"

Bryce nodded.

Clark's eyes sparkled. "We know how much Republicans love their tax breaks. From what we understand, you have quite a hefty tax bill due this year. Join forces with us and we will wipe that out for you. And that's just one minor example of how we *might* help each other."

4

Halloween 1996

Florent was sure Athena was dead.

Her mangled body was twisted in awkward directions and oozed blood. Florent could see broken skin, fractured bones.

It's happening again, he thought. *I'm going to lose Athena like I lost my father.*

A crowd amassed around him. People screamed when they saw Athena in the street. Someone was on the phone with 911.

"Is she your girlfriend?" a woman asked. "I was in the taxi that—"

She couldn't bring herself to finish the sentence.

Inside Florent's chest, words knocked around like raw gems in a rock tumbler. Could he bring himself to speak again as he had moments ago, when he called out Athena's name?

It felt like it took forever for the ambulance to come.

Was it hours? Of course not. Surely only minutes had passed.

As the EMTs rushed to help, they announced that Athena had a pulse after an initial, brief examination. Her eyes even fluttered open for a few seconds. However, she wasn't conscious long enough to say anything. Florent observed the scene, feeling as though he was watching an episode of *ER* rather than experiencing these horrible events himself.

He shivered and his teeth chattered. Wishing he could move closer, he found his body unable to, so he couldn't go near Athena. The truth was that he was afraid that at any second she might die, and he could not bear the thought of touching her corpse.

The EMTs suggested taking Athena to the trauma center at Manhattan Medical on the Lower East Side, and Florent nodded in agreement. He scuttled into the back of the ambulance and rode alongside her as she lay on the stretcher.

He was dazed, and his thoughts chattered away.

People die. Dying is part of life. I nearly died. How long does it take for a body to turn cold? Will Athena turn blue? Why didn't I die in St. Moritz? That would have been easier, cleaner. Will my life be an endless series of disasters and struggles forever? Will bad luck follow me for the rest of my life?

Oddly, he found himself missing Gia. He imagined stepping out of the ambulance and spotting her behind the glass door of the hospital's ER. He fantasized that he would run to her and fall into her arms, sobbing. If only Gia could have loved him, maybe everything would have been different.

5

April 12th

Gia's burner phone buzzed on the dresser. She bounced baby Serena onto her hip and grabbed the phone with one hand.

"*Pronto,*" she said, answering the call.

"*Buongiorno, Signorina Acquaviva,*" replied *La Nonna,* on the other end of the line.

"Donatella, what news do you have for me today?"

"It appears that the leader of your hard men is in town this evening."

"Shadow is in Paris?"

"Indeed, and he would like to meet you at your club."

"How strange. La Perle Noire is closed."

"No, apparently tonight it will reopen. Shadow gave me a full report this morning. His men have been working with your friend Dimitri around the clock to get everything back in order."

Gia paused for a moment, taking in the new information. "How can he possibly turn things around so quickly? It has only been a week since he began working on my case."

"Perhaps he wants to flex his muscles and impress you."

"Hmm," Gia murmured. "Maybe. Do you have an update for me regarding Vittore?"

"*Signorina Acquaviva,* I have nothing but the best news for you this morning. He will arrive in less than a week. With Shadow's help, I have arranged to bring Vittore directly to you."

"*Grazie,* Donatella! That is wonderful!" Gia sang as she realized that this was one of the first times she had been truly pleased with her fixer.

* * *

GIA WAS in the shower when Florent arrived at the hideaway on the Île Saint-Louis. He rapped on the door to make his presence known and then pushed it open.

"Did you miss me?" he asked. "I wonder what kind of trouble you got up to with two full weeks on your own?"

"What do you think?" Gia replied, winking.

He admired her from afar. Her long, dark hair fell behind her shoulders. His eyes swept over her whole body. They lingered on her light pink nipples and the shock of dark fuzz between her thighs. He wanted to bury himself between her legs immediately.

He smirked at her as he approached the marble shower. "Is there room in here for me?"

She slid the door open and pulled him in with all his clothes on.

"This isn't what I meant!" he fussed, annoyed as the water washed over him.

"Shhh," she whispered, loosening his tie. She peeled off every piece of his now soaked clothing and tossed it over the wall into the bathtub. But the tie stayed in her hands.

"Kneel down," she commanded.

Florent turned his head to the side, eyeing her with great suspicion. "I give the orders around here."

"Not this evening, *amore.*"

It took a little while, and some groping on Gia's behalf, but finally, he obliged her, lowering himself onto his knees. The rain panels in the ceiling above covered him with a soft pattering of warm water. He felt instantly relaxed and very aroused.

Gia tugged the tie along his shoulders and tickled it across the scar on his neck. That horrible, beautiful scar.

"Do you trust me?" Gia purred.

Florent burst out laughing at the inquiry. "No, of course not. Do you expect me to?"

She ignored the question and pressed on. "Let me blindfold you."

"And then what? Toss me into the Seine with a brick attached to my feet?"

"Be serious, Florent." Gia spread her legs wide, exposing herself to him. "If you want me, you must let me have my way."

His lips parted as he peeked between Gia's thighs. In his mind, he could already taste her. "Fine," he relented. "Do your worst."

She knotted the silk tie around his head, covering his eyes. "Open your mouth."

He did.

She reached between her legs and buried two fingers inside herself for a moment. Then she slid them over his tongue.

He let out a little gasp.

She leaned down and kissed him, cradling his cheeks in her hands. There was something different about the way she was touching him—there was a tenderness present that he hadn't felt before. His heart offered a little electric jolt, and he tensed up.

"Put your head in my lap, Florent," she purred quietly.

Gia guided his head on top of her thighs, and she stroked his hair. Her fingers tip-toed across his scar, and she felt something unusual... she felt sad.

She thought about Riley's offer to kill Florent, and she realized that she didn't want him to die. Melancholy rushed over her as she realized she would miss him.

"I love you," she said, not meaning to.

She froze.

The words had dropped out of her mouth by accident. And as

soon as they had, she felt a heaviness in her chest. She wasn't sure if it was regret, nostalgia, or guilt. Perhaps a cocktail made from each of those emotions.

What is happening to me? She'd suddenly lost her confidence and gone all panicky.

Florent lifted the blindfold. Even though water dripped down his face, his eyes were wet with tears.

"I love you, too, Gia"

* * *

Gia and Florent breezed through the stage door of La Perle Noire holding hands. The scene behind the curtain of the club was organized chaos. Dimitri shouted orders, keeping everyone in line. Gia felt as though she'd slipped through a crack in time and landed back twenty-five years ago.

Dimitri approached the couple with some trepidation, eyeing both of his former lovers with suspicion.

"*Ciao!*" Gia said, smiling. "Hurry up and kiss me hello, Dimitri. We have a show to see!"

Dimitri hovered in place for a moment, seemingly in disbelief, and finally allowed himself to offer a sincere welcome. "I feel as though no time has passed," he admitted, throwing his arms around her.

She embraced her old friend with a ferocity she wasn't expecting to feel. "You disappeared, Dimitri. Apart from Valentine's Day when you introduced Sade at the private performance, I have not seen you in years."

Dimitri hung his head. "Many unfortunate things have happened to me over the years, Gia. I'm sorry I was not present in your life, but that's a conversation for another time."

"Everything is fine," Florent interjected, patting Dimitri on the back. "I found you, Dimitri, and you are here now."

Dimitri smiled, "My favorite threesome, back together again after all this time."

Immediately, Florent's bemused look drooped, and he became serious. "Things between the three of us will not be as it was before," he hissed. "Do you understand me, Dimitri?"

Dimitri stumbled backwards, his mood immediately changed. "Please excuse me. It is almost showtime."

Florent readjusted himself and then turned to face Gia. "Where is Shadow?"

"How would I know?" she shrugged. She scoped out the room, checking out the many unfamiliar faces. There were muscular men stationed around the club, particularly at all the entrances. "Florent, you are the one who knows the man. Point him out to me when you see him."

Florent frowned. "I don't really *know* him. We have worked together for many years, but I have never met him in person."

"No? Then why has he asked to meet me face-to-face tonight?"

"Perhaps he doesn't trust you, Gia. Perhaps he has never met a mermaid. Why don't you ask him?"

Gia eyed Florent with a sour expression. "I do not need lessons in how to make conversation, Florent. *Grazie.*"

"Let's not fight, please."

"I am not arguing. I asked you a logical question, and you became... insolent, as you usually do."

Florent winced. Her insults always cut him deeply.

They walked in silence to the owner's booth. When they turned the corner, they saw that a man was already seated at their table.

"That must be Shadow," Gia noted.

The man stood as Gia neared the table. He was a very tall Black man with a solid build and wide shoulders. He sported a high fade, and his hair was lightly salt-and-peppered. His closely trimmed grey goatee showed more of his age.

"So this is the famous Gia Acquaviva," he observed aloud.

"And you must be Shadow," she replied.

He grinned a little. "That's me. Always lurkin' about and darkest at mid-day." His voice was deep and raspy, with a thick East London accent.

He put his hand out to shake hers.

"*Incantata*," she said, as their hands met.

Gia was not a petite woman, but her hand inside Shadow's looked tiny. This made her feel as though there was a power imbalance.

As if reading her mind, Shadow reassuringly whispered, "I like a firm handshake. It's a sign of a good head for business."

"Shall we sit?" She motioned to her table.

"After you," Shadow said, letting her slide in first.

Florent hung back, leering at them. He felt his chest flushing. He swallowed a few times and chewed on the inside of his cheek.

Shadow finally turned toward Florent. "Mr. Bisset, won't you join us?"

Florent put out his own hand, but Shadow offered his fist for a bump instead. Shadow's movements were suave, which made Florent feel awkward. Florent ended up putting his palm over Shadow's fist, awkwardly dipping it down twice.

They settled into the booth, Gia situated between the two men.

As Florent analyzed the handsome, manly man in front of him, he could barely contain his insecurity. "The elusive Shadow. A man of mystery," he huffed. Then he lobbed a verbal grenade at Shadow, hoping to throw him off his game. "Shouldn't you be out managing your henchmen? I would have thought that you would be far too busy to be hanging out in a cabaret."

"Me *henchmen*?" Shadow scoffed. "You make it seem as if I should be pulling on my beard like a Bond villain."

Gia waved her hand in her lover's direction. "Pay no mind to Florent," Gia said, overtly flirting with Shadow. "I think he is envious that he has not had the pleasure of meeting you until now."

Florent recoiled, leaning his shoulders against the banquette. "You bring up a good point, Gia. Shadow... why is it that we have not met?"

Shadow bared a wide smile. His top teeth were perfectly straight, but the bottom ones were somewhat snaggled. "My apologies, Mr. Bisset, but you never asked."

Neither had Gia, but Florent didn't see the point in pressing the issue further.

"Shall we order a bottle of champagne?" Florent asked Gia.

"Apologies again, Mr. Bisset," Shadow interrupted. "I don't drink."

"How unfortunate for you," Florent snapped.

"Not really. Don't like it. Makes me mind swayze."

"Swayze?" Florent asked, not understanding what Shadow meant.

"Patrick Swayze... lazy. It's rhyming slang."

Florent gawped at Shadow. "I don't remember you speaking in rhymes and riddles all these years that I have worked with you."

"Then maybe you wasn't listening, mate."

6

April 14th

While Mariama slept in the guest wing at Langley Manor, Awa went for a nice dip in the Hudson River. East of the valley, the sun stretched to life. Awa flicked through the strong currents in the river like a warm knife through butter.

She passed an old man fishing from a pontoon boat and waved at him. He nearly capsized out of shock. Never in his seventy-nine years had he seen a mermaid—and certainly not a Black mermaid sporting hot pink hair that matched her hot pink tail.

When Awa returned to the house, she saw that the chef had laid out fresh juice, fruit, and croissants in the breakfast room. Mariama descended the manor's elegant staircase and kissed her wife good morning.

"This is the life!" Mariama said, as she bit into a croissant. "I'm feeling very retired, and I very much love it." She smiled and sighed. "Oh! And Moussa called and asked you to ring him back."

Awa nodded, placed some fresh fruit on a plate, and stepped out the side door. She headed in the direction of Bronwyn's former cottage, which Awa had commandeered and made into her war head-quarters.

Logging onto the secure server, Awa dialed Moussa for a video conference.

When he answered, she greeted him graciously. "Good Morning, Your Majesty."

Moussa flipped his locs over his shoulder with pride. "I'll never get used to you calling me that, *Maman*."

"What is the business of the day?" she inquired.

"Kyle told me that the FBI has lured Bryce in as an informant."

"So they've flipped him?" Awa practically shouted, her eyebrows shooting up on her forehead.

"It seems so."

"Hmmm," Awa pondered, "I doubt very much that he will truly turn on Queen Karen. Did Kyle say who Bryce spoke to at the FBI?"

"No, he didn't mention that."

"Next time you speak, get as much detailed information as you can. But be careful, because you can't trust Kyle," Awa warned.

"He's on *our* side, *Maman*," Moussa pressed, his thoughts briefly turning to their recent *rendezvous*.

Awa waved an impatient hand at the screen. "Oh, Moussa, please! Don't let a little nookie cloud your judgment. He stood by and let his mother slaughter our people. Never forget that."

"Believe me, I could never forget what happened. I'm the one down here in Brazil dealing with the aftermath."

"How is the tension with the Sugarloaves?"

Moussa let out a frustrated sigh. "Everything would be a lot smoother here if we could get an infusion of cash from Gia. Every day there seems to be some conflict over having to feed and house us for free. We need to slice away at our tab with João and then pay our own way."

"I'll speak to Gia. Ah... also, I have an interesting development for you. Something unexpected."

"Do tell."

"Gia's former publicist got in touch with me yesterday...Talia Levy.

She's interested in taking us on as her clients. She mentioned securing an agent and *endorsement deals*."

"So, you're telling me that Hollywood has finally come calling?" Moussa laughed, his eyes lighting with fresh excitement.

"I don't know about Hollywood yet, but certainly Manhattan is on the line."

7

Halloween 1996

Florent stared at the payphone in the hospital's waiting room. He knew what he needed to do, but could he do it?

He put his hand on his throat, feeling the curved spine of his scar on his palm. He swallowed. Then he summoned a sound, a groan. It was mostly air at the start, a light whistle if anything. He pushed with more force from his chest and his diaphragm, and the noise became louder.

"Ahhh...theeee...naaaa," he managed to croak.

He hacked a ragged cough from the effort of it all.

Summoning all of his strength, he headed for the payphone.

He picked up the receiver and dialed Information. He'd only ever seen people do this in American movies, so it felt strange.

"Di...ana Paaa...paaa...do...nissss."

"Would you like me to put you through?" asked the operator.

"Yes," he said, whispering.

After about three rings, Athena's mother answered. "Hello?"

"Flo...rent."

"Florent? Is that you?" she replied, worry immediately present in her voice. "Oh, God. What's happened?"

"Ahhh...theeee...naaaa."

"What? Where is my baby?"

"Hossss...piii—"

"Hospital? Is that what you said? Oh, God. Which one, Florent?"

"Mannn...hatttt—"

"Manhattan Medical? No! Oh, my God. Stay there. I'm on my way."

Placing the receiver back on its cradle, Florent used the last of his remaining energy to shuffle over to a chair. He crumpled into himself and waited.

8

April 16th

"Come to *Nonno*," Vittore cooed, stretching his arms out for Serena.

Gia stood in the driveway with her hands on her hips. "And what about me? Ah? Do I even get a simple hello, *Methusalamme*?"

"Later! Later!" He cradled Serena and kissed her head.

Shadow hung back inside the black car that had driven Vittore through the gates of the Paris hideaway.

Gia sashayed over to the car's window to speak with him. "Shadow, *grazie mille* for bringing *Methusalamme* to see me. I have been waiting so long... too long... to spend time with this old man."

"Think nothing of it, Gia." Shadow tipped his cap to her. "Now, I better be running along. Skulls won't crack themselves, and we got a casino in Monte Carlo that needs a change in management."

"You have no idea what joy it brings my heart to hear that," Gia said, beaming. "After that, I want you to focus on regaining control of my casino in Venice."

"As you wish, Gia. Soon you'll be back to making serious bees and honey."

Gia's brow furrowed. "Sorry, I do not understand. What is that?"

"Bees and honey... money, money!" Shadow replied with a smirk, rubbing his fingers together.

Gia nodded her head, feeling slightly awkward, because, for some reason, she didn't really want Shadow to go. She stood back and smiled at him, waving as the car window rolled up.

"That is a delightful man," Vittore noted.

"I like him," Gia said, turning to face Vittore.

Vittore elbowed Stavros in the ribs. "We can see that, can we not, Stavros? Flirty, flirty!"

Gia shook her head, dispelling the notion. "The relationship is strictly business. Let's go inside."

When Gia popped open the double doors and led the couple into the spacious foyer, Vittore gawked at the high ceilings and fine details of the old home.

"The Frenchie?" Vittore asked. "What is his name? He must be in love with you if he sets you up in a home like this for free."

Gia offered him a sideways glance. "Florent and I have a long history."

Vittore made bug eyes at Stavros. "History, hmmm."

They all sat down in the living room, and Vittore held onto Serena so tightly, hugging her and sniffing her blonde curls. "You must stop growing, *bambina*. I need to enjoy my grandchild being a baby a little longer!" Then he turned to Gia. "*Tesoro mio*, come to me." She eased down onto the sofa beside him, and he embraced her, too. "My girls! My girls! How much I have missed you." Vittore's eyes got misty, and then he said, "When will you come back to Venice, Gia? I want to be near you and Serena."

"Now that the Langleys are gone, I no longer face the issues with custody. The media seem to now be focused on Awa and the war. But I still have a lot to do to get my businesses functioning again, and I think Venice is not a good place for this. I need to dash in and out without so many headaches. I am thinking of staying in Switzerland for a while."

"Switzerland?" A voice boomed from behind Gia. She turned her head to see that Florent had entered the room.

"*Amore!*" She rose to kiss Florent hello. "I was not expecting you this afternoon."

"And yet, *here I am*," he replied, his lips tight.

"Florent," Gia grabbed him by the hand and led him over to the sofa, "this is Vittore and his fiancé Stavros."

Vittore passed Serena to Gia and then hugged Florent, hanging onto him as he spoke. "Thank you for everything you have done to help my Gia. Stavros was part of the operation that saved Gia from that evil man in Sicily. You, too, helped save her life back then. And now, coming to her aid again with this house and everything... ah! I will be forever grateful to you, Son!"

Florent wasn't expecting such a show of emotion, and he wiggled nervously in Vittore's embrace. "Gia and I have a long history."

Vittore wrinkled his bushy, white eyebrows and replied, "That is *exactly* what my Gia said about *you*."

Gia leaned in. "If you do not mind, gentlemen, there is a very important topic we must discuss... the wedding! Stavros, what are you thinking?"

"Bah!" Vittore jumped in. "I am the bride! That old goose has been married before."

Stavros winked at Vittore. "You are right, my young lover. This is your moment to shine, so I will gladly do anything that makes you happy."

Gia reached out and squeezed Stavros's hand. "I am so happy you are both here. Truly."

"I have a surprise for all of you," Florent announced. "To celebrate this happy occasion, I have arranged for catering from the most expensive restaurant in Paris, Guy Savoy. Unfortunately, I have other plans this evening, so I will not join you, but please enjoy yourselves in my absence. I know there is much to discuss."

* * *

AFTER DINNER, Vittore insisted on having the *au pair* move Serena's crib into his bedroom. "Serena and I need to make up for lost time, *tesoro mio*," he explained to Gia, who was more than happy to oblige Vittore.

After showering and climbing into bed, Gia heard a familiar tapping at her window.

"Shhh," Gia whispered as she opened the window for Riley. "I have guests in the house."

Riley wrapped her arms around Gia, covering her in kisses.

"How much longer will you be in Paris?" Gia asked.

"About a week, and then I head to Switzerland to shoot some scenes for the movie. They're teaching me to rock climb. I wish you could see me in the parkour studio. I'm like Spiderman!"

Gia smiled at this news. "What a coincidence. I am also planning to go to Switzerland for a while."

"No fucking way! I'll be in Davos. You?"

"St. Moritz. I have a chalet there, but it is rented, so I will stay at Château Gelé."

"Oh, shit! I think that's really close to the studio... an hour's drive or so." Riley pushed Gia's hair over her ear. "So, we can make this a more regular thing, huh?"

"Perhaps," Gia answered, biting her lip.

"You kill me when you bite your lip like that. Gimme." She devoured Gia's lips, biting and sucking them. After that, she moved onto Gia's neck.

"Do not leave any marks," Gia commanded. "I cannot have Florent seeing that."

"Fuck Florent." Riley pushed Gia onto the bed and proceeded to give Gia a nice hickey, right at the base of her neck.

Riley had become even stronger and more muscular with all the training for the film. She easily moved Gia around in the bed. Turning Gia over onto her stomach, Riley stripped off Gia's bathrobe.

Then she ran her hands down Gia's back, stopping to fondle Gia's ass, before diving in between Gia's legs.

Gia moaned into a pillow as Riley slowly put more and more fingers inside of her. Riley pressed her pelvis against Gia's hips in a rhythm, so that the force of her hand was magnified. It felt so good. Riley's hands filled up the space inside Gia perfectly, touching every inch of her, exciting all the erotic places within.

"Do not stop," Gia begged. "I am so close."

But Riley did stop. She turned Gia over onto her back and kissed her hard. "Come in my mouth," Riley ordered.

Riley once again entered Gia, and this time put her mouth over Gia's clit. They moved together on the bed, Gia sliding slightly over the edge, her head hanging off. Gia felt herself start to come, and then—

The bedroom door creaked open.

Gia's eyes glanced up to see Vittore, upside down. He was holding Serena in his arms, and his mouth dropped.

"Father in the Sky! Oh my!" Vittore squealed.

Just as quickly as he had come in, Vittore scuttled out, slamming the door behind him.

Riley lifted her head from between Gia's legs.

"What happened?" Riley asked. She had been so focused on Gia that she missed the whole interaction with Vittore.

"I will be right back," Gia said. "Stay here."

Gia scampered to the bathroom, washed her face, and then threw on her robe. She tiptoed down the hall to Vittore's room.

He answered the door with a red face. "I am sorry. I should have knocked. Who is that?"

"Her name is Riley. We have been seeing each other."

"Does Florent know about this?"

"*Methusalamme,* do not be so old-fashioned."

"That is not an answer to my question."

"No, Florent does not know."

"So you have been carrying on an affair under this man's nose after everything he has done to help you? What is *wrong* with you, Gia? Have you no shame?"

Gia's face burned hot. She hated disappointing Vittore. Worse, she had nothing to say for herself. Of course, she had no shame. In fact, the deception was a huge turn-on.

"I do not understand, Gia, why you turn away from love every time it presents itself to you. I believe that Florent loves you. His actions explain this. Why would you disrespect him in this way?"

Gia felt herself growing angry at the reprimand. She was not a child. She was a grown woman—one who would not be beholden to any man. Suddenly, she lashed out.

"Why can you not see things from my point of view... be on *my* side?"

"*Sirenetta*, I am on your side! But I will not stand by and say nothing as you break this man's heart and squander another chance at happiness."

"Excuse me, *Methusalamme*," she huffed, "but you are not my father. Do not speak to me this way!"

Vittore stumbled backward, losing his balance. "I am *not your father?*" He held his hand over his chest. "How dare you! I do not even know what to say to you. Please go," he demanded, closing the door in her face.

Gia was devastated. Inside, another version of herself was shrieking and smashing a brick wall with a sledgehammer.

This had not turned out to be the night she had imagined.

9

April 18th

"And we're back," Harper said into the camera, speaking to her OTN viewers. "Tonight I'm joined by Iris Cutler, the head of the re-election campaign for our former United States President, Ronnie Spade. Good evening, Iris."

Iris flashed a bleached smile. "Happy to be here, Harper. I'm a huge fan."

Harper plastered on a fake grin and then angled herself between her B camera and the show's second guest. "Also joining us is the CEO of Animals Deserve Equal Treatment, Alicia Alvarez. Welcome to the show, Alicia. I'll admit that I never imagined I would be hosting a vegan propagandist on Prime Time, but here we are."

"Oh, Harper, I know you don't eat red meat," Alicia clapped back. "I read that profile they did of you in *Shape* Magazine. Honestly, you should take the leap and switch to a fully plant-based diet. I make a killer vegan *pernil* that would rock your world."

Harper wagged her finger. "I could never live without shrimp. And... speaking of sea creatures, I would like to turn our attention to Karen Dean of the California mermaid colony. Queen Karen has been on the run from the FBI for several weeks now. I can confirm exclusively that Prince Bryce Dean, who is in custody at the moment, has cut a deal with the authorities to rat out his mother." Harper turned to Iris. "Ms. Cutler, what do you think about that?"

"Harper," Iris crowed, "I'm not sure why you keep covering this mermaid *crap* when there are everyday Americans out there struggling to make ends meet with record-high levels of inflation. The President is really disappointed in your coverage."

"If I may," interrupted Alicia, cutting in, "*Ex-President* Spade took large campaign donations from Karen Dean, did he not?"

Iris shook her head. "Not that I am aware of."

"Mmm," Alicia sucked her teeth, "then he must not be keeping you very well informed, because we have paperwork that shows the transactions. We've given it to Harper."

"It's true," Harper echoed. "Let's pull up the proof."

The screen behind Harper showed an enlarged image that featured a stack of wire transfer confirmations.

Harper read from the monitor. "Our financial analysts here at OTN have traced the wires and determined that Queen Karen Dean provided Ronnie Spade's election campaign with millions of dollars. It's all there in black and white. No denying it."

Iris shrugged. "Like I said, I was unaware of this. But it's not that surprising, considering the President's interest in environmental issues."

Harper sputtered, laughing. "Sorry, his... interest in *environmental issues*? Since when? Ronnie Spade goes golfing every Friday with oil tycoons. Are you seriously going to sit here and tell me he cares about the *ocean* being polluted?"

Alicia leaned forward, putting her elbows on the news desk. "Our confidential source told us that Queen Karen Dean received assurance from the ex-president that he would secure a special tax credit for her colony... which by the way is technically not even in the United States... but rather floating in International Waters."

Iris smiled, before shrugging again. "You are both full of surprises tonight."

Harper looked down the barrel of the camera lens. "It will be interesting to see what transpires in the Mermaid Civil War. It's apparent that Karen Dean has made enemies in the current U.S. administration... but seems also to have made the former president a close ally."

10

April 19th

Days had passed, and Vittore still refused to speak to Gia. If Florent was there, he would play nice and pretend everything was fine, but the moment they were alone again, Vittore went back to sulking and giving her the cold shoulder.

"You leave tomorrow, Vittore," Gia stated matter-of-factly. "Are you planning to waste the rest of the time we have together pouting like a little boy?"

"Stavros," Vittore said, tilting his head, "do you hear a cricket? There is an *eeep eeeep eeeeeep* sound buzzing in my ear."

"Enough!" Stavros yelled, slamming his hand on the kitchen counter. "I will not allow the two of you to continue fighting like this. We have too many items to discuss about the wedding. Now, please, hug and make up."

Gia approached Vittore with open arms, but he held his hand out in front of him. "No, no. I will not move forward with you until you apologize."

"I am sorry!" Gia cried.

"About?" Vittore insisted, demanding a more elaborate *mea culpa*.

Gia reached out and took his hand. "I should not have insulted you."

"*Because?*" Vittore pushed her for more details.

Gia exhaled a frustrated sigh. "All of my life you have cared for me. You were there after both my parents died, and you have always loved me with your whole heart and treated me like a daughter. Believe me, *Methusalamme*, I am so grateful to have you. I love you more than I love myself, and you know that! Now, let me embrace you, you old mule!"

Gia closed the space between her and Vittore, and he let her hug him. He squeezed her tightly. "You are too thin. I can feel your bones. You need to eat some pasta, Gia!"

She rolled her eyes and poured three mimosas. "I would like to make a toast," she announced, raising her glass. "To the most wonderful couple in the world. I wish you every happiness."

Stavros hugged them both and then rubbed Vittore's cheek before kissing him.

"I am so happy, my young lover," Stavros whispered to Vittore.

Vittore was misty-eyed, as usual. "My dear family, all together in one place."

* * *

THAT NIGHT, Florent came for dinner and stayed over. He laid in bed next to Gia and she rested her head on his chest. She discovered his heart was racing.

"Is something wrong?" she asked. "Your heart is beating so fast."

"I don't want you to go to Switzerland," Florent replied. "I have gotten used to having you in Paris... and I am afraid that if I let you leave, I will never see you again."

She lifted her head to see that Florent had his eyes squeezed shut. "*Tsk, tsk, amore.* I do not like to see you so upset." She kissed him. "What silly nonsense. I will be in St. Moritz, not at the bottom of the ocean. You have a jet... you can come and see me anytime you wish."

"If you break my heart, Gia... I swear... I'll...I'll..." Florent could not bring himself to threaten her this time. The thought of anything bad happening to her—even something he might have orchestrated himself—hurt him too much. He grabbed her hand and placed it over his heart. "You live in here, inside me. You always have. I have loved you since I met you, Gia. You have been my singular torment and also my muse. I cannot stand losing you again. I would rather die."

Gia giggled. "Florent! What dramatics. *Amore*, I assure you, your heart is in good hands."

"Unfortunately," he mumbled, "I know that is not true."

She shook her head at him. "I do not know what to say."

"Promise me that you belong only to me."

"I belong..." she hesitated.

"Only to me!" Florent's face was turning red, anger flashed in his eyes. "*Say it.*"

"You are so possessive, honestly. I do not care for this part of your personality at all."

Florent narrowed his eyes at her, knowing that he could ruin her life if he wanted to. He considered reminding her of it, but he knew that such a statement would not bring about the declaration of fealty that he so desperately wanted.

"Do you even love me?" he asked.

"I have told you so, have I not?"

Florent turned his head and stared out the window at the Seine.

"Gia, if you love me like you claim you do, then why don't I believe you?"

11

November 1996

For Florent, Athena's first few days in the hospital melted together for him in a sort of trauma fog. He barely slept. He wasn't even allowed to see Athena for the entire first day of her stay. Diana tried to pry information about her daughter's condition from the doctors, but all they said at the beginning was, "We're running tests."

The doctors patched up Athena's body slowly. Her leg required surgery to install pins in order for it to heal. But Athena's brain was not recovering the way the medical team wanted it to.

After many scans, the doctors finally broke the news, "Severe brain damage."

"How severe?" Diana inquired. She leaned on Florent, because she thought that at any moment, her legs might give out.

The head doctor flipped through her chart and then glanced up at Diana. "We won't know unless she wakes up."

"Is there a chance she *won't* wake up?" Diana was in full panic mode now.

"Let's take it step by step." Then the doctors left Athena's hospital room.

Diana dissolved into tears. Florent wrapped his arms around her and let the woman soak his sweater with her sorrow.

He blew air out of his lips in a quiet whistle. "Shhh. Shhh."

After a few minutes, Diana had calmed down, wiping the wetness from her face. "You should go to the house and get some rest, Florent."

She wouldn't let him argue. Before he knew it, Diana had packed him into her Rolls Royce with her driver, sending him to her odd, sprawling mansion on Long Island.

12

April 23rd

"What about a collab with Gucci?!" Talia Levy asked Queen Awa. She scribbled ideas onto a whiteboard in her NYC office. Talia's office occupied the ground floor of a chic West Village brownstone, and she lived on the second and third stories. You see, Public Relations brought in the big bucks, especially with Talia's client roster.

Moussa, who was joining via Zoom, chimed in, in response to Talia's question. "You do know I'm a designer, right?"

"STOP IT RIGHT NOW!" Talia squealed. "Meant. To. Be!"

"I always knew the spotlight would find me," Moussa declared, his excitement causing him to involuntarily shimmy. "Lately I have been experimenting with kelp leather."

"Oooooh," Talia gasped. "We love a sustainability story, honey! Oh, I've got a fab idea... what if we propose designing a line of accessories made entirely out of plastic discarded in the ocean?"

"Mmmm..." Moussa frowned. "I'm not sure that I want my *entrée* into the world of *haute couture* to be associated with *trash*, Talia. Think chic. More Chanel... less... ugh... Balenciaga."

"Interesting," Talia replied. She turned to Awa with a big smile. "He has a real point of view, Queen, doesn't he?"

Awa nodded. "He has always said he's the next Karl Lagerfeld."

"But with Ralph Lauren's mass marketing skills!" Moussa added.

Talia took a seat at the head of the conference room table. "I just knew this was going to be a perfect fit. Now, let's talk numbers."

Awa and Moussa exchanged a worried glance.

Talia shuffled through some papers in a leather binder, passing Awa a stapled retainer agreement. "My starting fee is twenty thousand dollars a month."

Moussa swallowed hard; he felt a lump find a home in his throat.

"Talia," Awa began, "The attack on our colony has left us—"

"A little short on cash," Moussa finished his mother's sentence.

Talia's shoulders dropped. "That's a shame."

"What about a contingency agreement?" Awa proposed.

Talia grimaced. "That kind of thing... TBH... I haven't had good luck with percentages."

"Listen," Awa said, leaning in, "you will never in your life meet two more hardworking individuals than my son and myself. The stories I have to tell... you would scarcely believe them. I've been alive for over two hundred years, darling, and I know *a lot*. Remember how shocking it was for everyone to discover that Opal Windspray was a mermaid?"

"Yeah, of course." Talia's eyes were the size of two dessert plates.

Awa leaned way back in her chair, stringing out the drama. "Wait until the public learns about all the global leaders who are merfolk. A-list celebrities. Fortune 500 CEOs. The world might be a big place, but when it comes to power, I am paddling in a tiny pond. Understand?"

"Woah," Talia whispered. "I'm like... dead. Deceased. I cannot. You are blowing my freaking mind right now!"

"I have kept quiet for centuries, but I am now retired from my queenly duties, and I am ready to write a tell-all *for the ages*."

Talia covered her mouth with her hands for a second before speaking again. "Fucking epic!" She jumped out of her seat and bopped over to Awa. "Up, up, up!" Talia took Awa by both hands and raised her up from the table. "Let's do this! I believe in you both. We're gonna make a killing."

* * *

IN HIS RIO DE JANEIRO apartment, Moussa shook himself a celebratory martini and removed a chilled glass from the freezer. Stories below his temporary luxury housing, the waves crashed onto Ipanema Beach. He sighed to himself as he took a sip of his cocktail.

There are worse places to live in exile than sunny Brazil, he thought. *But I miss home.*

There was a knock at the door. Moussa pulled out a second frozen glass and poured another drink, balancing one in each hand as he made his way to the front door.

"It's open!" he yelled.

Kyle Dean peeked his normally blonde head through the front door, revealing a fresh copper dye job.

Moussa gasped. "Oh, my Gracious Tides! What have you *done* to your hair?"

"You like?" Kyle asked, shuffling in.

"No," Moussa admitted, shoving the martini toward Kyle. "I do *not* like it. You look like Prince Harry."

Kyle lifted Moussa's locs and kissed him on the neck. "Prince Harry's sexy, right?"

Moussa snorted. "Only if you're Meghan Markle." He shook his head in confusion. "What possessed you to do this to yourself?"

"It's to throw off anyone who might be following me."

Moussa locked and latched the door. "My, aren't you clever?"

"Don't tease me, Moussa. Come here and give me a kiss."

Moussa wrapped his arms around Kyle, and they kissed all the way into the bedroom, where they made love. Afterward, Moussa rested his head on the pillow next to Kyle's.

"Moussa, my mother is on her way to Greece to meet with Queen

Zale. I'm pretty sure she's plotting to kidnap Gia's baby and take her to the Archivist in Japan."

"Wait," Moussa sat straight up in bed. "*What?* Are you sure their meeting is about Serena and not simply strategizing about the war?"

"My mother tasked me with getting details about Gia's whereabouts."

"You can't tell her anything," Moussa insisted.

"I don't even know where Gia is. Do you?"

Moussa crossed his arms, considering this new information. "If I did, I wouldn't tell you."

"What the hell, Moussa? I'm being honest with you. Why would you hide anything from me?"

Moussa ignored the question and twisted one of his braids around his finger, pondering each angle. "I wonder... what does the Archivist want with Serena?"

"Togashi said something about not wanting Serena's power to be in the wrong hands. Apparently, she's some kind of prodigy with Ancient Magic."

Moussa's mind transported him back to the day that Serena brought him back to life. He had felt how strong she was even as he'd done everything he could to remain on the other side in Oumar's arms. Serena's pull had simply overwhelmed him.

I have to tell Gia that Karen is coming for Serena, he thought. *If Karen and Zale are going to be together, then we should launch an offensive attack.*

"I'm going to run down to the store," Moussa announced. "I'm out of vodka."

As soon as he was on the street, Moussa dialed his mother's number.

"*Maman*, we have a problem."

13

April 24th

Gia logged onto the secure server to find that Awa and Moussa were already waiting on the video call.

"*Buongiorno,*" Queen Mother Awa and King Moussa."

"Gia," Awa replied, jumping in immediately, "let me get right to the point. Queen Karen will be in Greece for the next two days. The purpose of her trip is to plan a kidnapping with Zale. They want Serena."

Gia's heart lurched, and her stomach dropped. "No, I will not allow that to happen."

"Of course not," Awa agreed. "That's why we need to strike now. If they're both going to be in Greece, that gives us the opportunity to attack the colony. If we are lucky, maybe we can take them both out."

Gia's mind raced, and she tried to quell her anxiety. "You are right. But how?"

"We need Bisset's help," Moussa explained. "Skirlor has a small group of Ice Folk who have agreed to travel to Greece to cast a spell, but we have to transport them from the Arctic Circle. We need a seaplane to fly and pick them up, and we need it *immediately*, or we will miss our chance."

"Can we not charter a plane?" Gia asked.

"No," Awa clarified, "not to Alert, Nunavut, in Canada. Commercial flights aren't allowed. Florent's planes will be allowed in, because they carry cargo."

Gia pounded her fist on the table. "*Merda!* I hate these women. Will I never know peace again?"

"Focus, please, Gia," Moussa begged. "We have lost so much already by defending you. We must see this through. You have to be strong. I hate Karen and Zale more than you, but I cannot allow that to cloud my reasoning. You have to secure Florent's help immediately."

Gia exhaled an uneven breath. "I understand."

* * *

WITHIN THE HOUR, Gia had called Florent to her hideaway on the Seine. He dropped everything and came running.

When he arrived, she immediately dialed Shadow and *La Nonna* from her burner phone.

"This is an emergency," she panted. "The women who attacked the colony in Dakar are after Serena. I do not know how they plan to kidnap her, but I need to get my baby to safety."

"Absolutely," Shadow crooned. "Rest easy. We will keep you both safe." His deep voice comforted her.

"That is not all." She reached out to touch Florent's cheek. "I need your help Florent. Desperately."

"Anything, Gia."

"We have some allies who are willing to attack the colony in Greece, but we must transport them from Northern Canada."

"Canada?" Florent repeated. "Hmm. I believe I have a cargo plane in Montreal at the moment."

"We need a seaplane."

He nodded, considering Gia's request. Then he pulled out his phone and began clicking around in his Bisset Industries app. "I have a fleet of seaplanes in Maine. There are two that are ready to leave at any time, but depending on the destination in Canada, they may need to stop for refueling."

"Florent, how quickly could we get everyone to Greece?" Gia asked.

"I have to run a logistics analysis. I cannot give you an exact answer right now. How long do we have?"

"Approximately forty-eight hours," she replied.

He nodded.

"*Ahem*," *La Nonna* cleared her throat. "Considering that we are all in Europe at the moment, would it not be easier simply to deal with this threat locally?"

Gia felt her shoulders tense up. "What do you mean by that?"

"I have a crew I can send to Greece," *La Nonna* explained. "The same boys who cleared out your death cavern, Gia."

"No," Gia scoffed. "There is no way that humans can find their way to the Greek colony alone. The entrance is too deep in the sea, and the path to arrive there is too complicated."

"Perhaps a submarine?" *La Nonna* joked.

"Please, Donatella. My daughter's life is in danger. I cannot bear your sense of humor today."

"Gia," Shadow said, "please stay with Mr. Bisset. I will be there in three hours to personally escort you to a safe house."

As they hung up the phone, the *au pair* brought Serena into the room. Gia took her child into her arms and hugged her close.

"Florent, close the shades and lock all the doors."

After doing as asked, Florent hurried back to be with Gia. He embraced both mother and daughter, kissing each of them on the head.

"*Mes anges*, my two angels," he whispered. He lifted his eyes and locked his gaze with Gia's. "Nothing will happen to you as long as I am with you." His lips met Gia's in a soft kiss. Florent felt Gia's spirit closer than ever, and his heart soared. He loved being needed by her.

Florent was proving to Gia once again that he would be there to catch her when she fell. She sensed that her heart was opening to him, because real trust was forming between the two of them. She laid her head on his shoulder, and she finally allowed herself to cry.

14

April 24th

Gia rode in the back of a small Bisset Industries cargo van, alongside Shadow. The rural local roads in Eastern France were bumpy, and all the motion had lulled Serena into a deep sleep.

"Are you usually so hands on with your clients?" Gia asked Shadow.

He chuckled. "You tellin' me that you ain't used to people going the extra mile with all that money you got? I woulda thought everyone bends over backwards for a billionaire. Especially one with your good looks."

"In general, I find people to be disappointing," Gia confessed. "How long will I stay at this safe house?"

"Try not to worry too much, Miss Mermaid." He winked at her, trying to put her at ease. "My team has everything under control, and Mr. Bisset is working on getting your warriors over to Greece."

Gia sighed. "I used to be very in control of every detail in my life. Now I feel as though I run from crisis to crisis with no long-term strategy."

"That's not true," he balked. "We already got your Paris club back, and your Monte Carlo casino. My boys will take over the Venice casino next week."

"What are you doing with all the Greek merfolk that Yiannis was using as staff?"

Shadow's eyes twinkled. "Are you sure you wanna know that?"

"Are you killing them?" Gia asked bluntly. Admittedly, after all the betrayal she had experienced by her own kind, she didn't care what he did with them.

He winked, "Nah. Let's call it... cold storage. They're all in the freezer for now."

"Impressive."

Shadow shrugged. "It's my job."

"When you capture my cousin Yiannis, I want you to tell me. Put him to the side, please. I would like to deal with him *personally*."

The van rolled to a stop, and the driver got out and opened the back door. Gia exited into a dark area, and she could tell by the echo of their footsteps that they were in a large place.

"Where are we?" she asked.

"Birthplace of painter Gustave Courbet," Shadow replied. "Ornans, France. I bought this stone mill ages ago. We got a small apartment inside set up for you. It's modest, but it has all you need."

Shadow led her through a dark hallway to a small studio apartment with a twin bed, a hot plate, and a space heater.

"Are you going now?" Gia inquired, hoping very much that his answer was no.

"I will stay with you as long as I am able, and then I want to take you to St. Moritz myself."

She glanced around the tiny room. "But where will you sleep?"

He reached under the twin bed and dragged out a small army cot, pointing to it.

Too bad, Gia thought. *Sharing a bed might have led to something interesting.*

* * *

Skirlor, Xenef, Frallon, and Thlood trekked across the icy flats of the Arctic Circle. The temperature was well below freezing, but these were the days of perpetual sunshine, so the journey was quite pleasant. The spring sunlight reflected off their translucent bodies like candlelight from a Venetian chandelier.

In the horizon, a seaplane came sputtering into view, landing on a patch of ground marked by a red-striped, blinking column.

The pilot opened the plane's door and yelled the codewords. "Is this the North Pole?"

Skirlor shouted his coded response. "You have arrived at Santa's workshop." Skirlor's voice was a rumbling shriek that set the pilot's hair on end.

The Ice Folk loaded into the plane and they took off into the cloudless sky.

15

November 1996

Athena had been in a coma for more than three weeks, waking only once, very briefly. That thirty-second break from darkness was enough to convince Florent to stay another week in New York, instead of returning to Europe as he had planned.

Yia Yia, Athena's grandmother, and Diana had organized themselves rather well, setting shifts so someone would always be at the hospital with Athena, in case she woke up. As time passed, Florent was finding his presence to be superfluous. However, he was speaking more regularly now, and while he still faced anxiety about getting his words out, Diana and Yia Yia insisted on paying for a speech pathologist to assist him. The sessions, admittedly, were helping a lot. No, he wasn't able to have full conversations yet, but he could answer questions here and there.

Sometimes when Diana was at the hospital, Florent would wander the halls of her mansion alone. He discovered a study—a grand library that had belonged to Athena's father, Adonis. The wooden cabinets were filled with treasures from the deep sea. Adonis purchased most of the items at auction, but there were a few artifacts that he had collected from the bottom of the ocean himself.

A huge chandelier, in the shape of a ship, lit the room. The ship's helm featured an impressive bronze mermaid. Florent stared at the chandelier for a long time, captivated.

Since he was all by himself, he didn't see the harm in poking around. He searched the room from top to bottom, looking for clues. Always tugging at the back of his mind was that improbable connection between Adonis and Gia's mother, Marina Acquaviva.

How was it possible that Marina was the last person to see Adonis before he disappeared? And *why* had Marina disappeared? Who was she? The woman seemed even more mysterious to him than her shadowy daughter, Gia.

He took every book off the shelf, flipped through the pages, and waited for clues to fall out. Nothing. He opened every drawer. Nothing. But he finally struck gold when he decided to check inside each and every old picture frame.

Inside a gold frame, underneath a photo of Adonis holding a large fish, was a weathered Polaroid photo.

The picture was of a young Adonis and a lovely redhead on a boat. Handwritten on the bottom of the Polaroid were the words, "Santorini, August 1969."

He stared at the redhead. He recognized her eyes, that was for sure. They were the same shape as Gia's. They held their heads the same way, and the likeness was undeniable.

This was her: He was looking at Marina Acquaviva.

16

April 25th

Queen Zale tipped a pitcher of seamilk, pouring the cool liquid into Queen Karen's hot tea. The women sat together in Queen Zale's private parlor inside her palace. Carved into the stone walls were relief sculptures of ancient Atargatic fables. One section of the frieze showed the Wrath of Amaterasu, the Japanese Goddess of the Sun. Karen inspected it, trying to remember details about the story her parents had told her long ago.

Zale noticed Karen admiring the artwork. "My grandmother etched the walls herself. She studied under the most talented artists of her day. She and the famous Greek sculptor Pheidias built this palace."

"Pheidias?" Karen asked. "That must have been a long time ago."

"Not so long... a little over two millennia."

Karen smirked. "Only you think in thousands of years and not decades, Queen Zale."

"When you have been alive as long as I have, time ceases being linear and begins to feel like a circle."

Queen Karen took a sip from her cup and then leaned back onto the settee. "Why do you suppose the Japanese want Gia's baby? What do you think they will do with her?"

"Let us be clear," Zale noted, growing stern, "it is only the Archivist who seeks to control the child. Togashi has failed to rewrite history and is now determined to influence the future. If the child truly is a conduit to Sky Magic, then Togashi will stop at nothing to harness that power."

"Do you think Togashi plans to harm Serena?"

"Is not the loss of one child worth regaining such rare and potent magic?" shrugged Zale, her voice flat and devoid of compassion.

Karen considered those words for a moment and then replied, "Perhaps you are right."

"Have you discovered any more information on the movements of Gia Acquaviva?" Upon mentioning Gia's name, Zale's whisper-soft voice developed a sharp edge.

"We are working on it," Karen replied.

Zale's mouth stretched into a sneer. "The woman is a pest. I should have exterminated her when I had the chance." Zale picked up a bell from the side table and rang for her assistant. When the servant entered the room, she said, "Summon Yiannis. We are ready for his counsel."

* * *

SKIRLOR and the Ice Folk reached the pearly sands of the Greek colony's *Nisí Margaritarión,* Pearl Island, shortly before nightfall. The foursome linked hands as they stood on the beach, forming a circle. They began chanting, and as their voices repeated the ancient spell, their breath became a fog. The frozen vapor converged, forming an intricately patterned web of ice. When they let go of one another, the newly formed sheet of ice dropped to the ground, spraying hundreds of shards across the sand.

Their enchantments were ready. It was time to attack.

The Ice Folk dove into the dark blue waters of the crescent bay and swam toward the main entrance of the Greek colony. Skirlor led the way through the convoluted system of aquatic tunnels and caves.

* * *

"BUT HOW CAN we smoke her out, Yianni?" Karen asked. Yiannis and the two queens had already been engaged in a strategy session regarding Gia for more than half an hour.

Yiannis cracked a sly smile. "I propose that we use the thing she cares about the most... money."

"Say more," Queen Zale demanded.

"I will use myself as a lure. Her team has already captured dozens of Greeks during her attempts to regain control of her empire. I could reach out, waving the white flag... tell her that things have gone far enough and I want to negotiate the handover of the rest of her holdings in person."

"The woman is intelligent," Queen Karen pointed out. "What if she doesn't believe you're sincere? Would she not just continue taking over the businesses one by one? Why does Gia need *you*?"

"Gia believes that I have betrayed her. She is a vindictive person, and I am sure she wants revenge. If she thinks she has a chance to get to me, that alone is enough to motivate her to come out of hiding."

Queen Zale nodded in agreement. "Excellent, I would like you to—"

Suddenly there was a loud ping on the window of the parlor room. Everyone's attention was drawn to the glass. A crack had formed in the window, and it was rapidly spreading, crackling like a fire with every new fissure.

Rumbling noises exploded all around them as the floor shook. They ran toward the door to the hallway, seeking safety, but before they could reach it, a giant ice spear came hurling through the window, landing at the heels of Queen Zale.

Yiannis threw himself in front of his queen. "Run, Your Majesty!"

Zale pushed him out of the way and screamed, "Get behind me!"

Raising both hands, she chanted wildly.

Water was pouring through the hole in the window, quickly filling up the room. Queen Zale's legs gave way to her tail. She thrashed against the current to stay in place.

Queen Karen spotted four figures in the water. Arrows made of ice shot through the water all around her. One snagged the edge of her tail, and she yelped in pain. She hid behind a heavy wooden door, just as a spray of arrows shot into it. She pulled one out, and it burned her finger with its shattering cold. Never had she witnessed the staggering power of Ice Magic.

Wasting no more time, Karen bolted down the corridor, attempting to escape, but she swam directly into a wall of transparent ice. The impact caused her to lose consciousness. Her body see-sawed in the current.

Back in the parlor, Queen Zale stood on her own, summoning the Spirit of the Sea. "O Gracious Tides," she sang, "I am your humble child. Wrap me in the cloak of your protection, O Voice of the Deep. Spare me from these evil forces."

Water bubbled around her, coiling like a snake, twisting her into the calm eye of an aquatic tornado. Every arrow shot in her direction was gobbled up and spit back. One pierced Thlood in the stomach and struck with such force that the merman was propelled to the bottom of the sea.

Skirlor, Xenef, and Frallon retreated.

However, Queen Zale was no longer in control of the spell. In fact, she was so disoriented that she curled into a ball inside the eye of the storm. In turn, the tornado bounced through the colony, wrecking everything in its path. The storm destroyed the beautiful carvings in the queen's parlor. And the residents of the colony fled in every direction as the walls crashed down around them.

Boulders came loose from the ceiling and closed off the corridor where Queen Karen was floating.

The tornado bounced through the hole created by the falling rocks. Queen Zale was carried along as the tornado raced with great speed in the direction of the most dangerous part of the sea: Cold Currents.

17

April 26th

G ia's burner phone buzzed to life on the bed beside her. She blinked her eyes open and answered the call, clicking the button to activate the speaker phone.

Shadow sat up in his cot, watching over Gia.

"*Pronto?*"

"It's Awa. I just heard from Skirlor. They succeeded in their attack. They lost Thlood, but they believe they took out Queen Karen. The colony caved in, and they say it's practically in ruins now. They are fairly certain Queen Zale also died in the collapse."

Gia was surprised that she felt sadness at the news. Not because of the queens, but because the colony was destroyed. Such a beautiful, wondrous place—her mind drifted to Cameron and his level of fascination at the underwater world. She wondered if her grandparents had made it out alive. And Yiannis? The colony was her ancestral home, and being a part of its destruction was a hollow victory, if anything.

"Awa," Gia muttered, "thank you for calling. I will ring you later, once I have had a chance to regroup with my team."

Serena woke up, and Gia gave her a bottle of seamilk so she wouldn't start crying.

Gia turned toward Shadow and asked, "What should we do now?"

"Nothing," he replied. "We wait."

Gia noticed a slew of unanswered text messages on her phone, all from Riley. At first, the messages were sweet and flirty. But after Gia failed to answer, Riley's tone had soured. It was now clear that Riley was furious that Gia had gone silent on her again. Gia's forehead creased as she thought about the unpleasantness she would have to deal with when she was face-to-face with Riley.

18

May 2nd

Queen Awa stepped out of Talia's Cadillac Escalade looking like a million bucks. They maneuvered through the star-struck crowds and entered the NASDAQ headquarters. A few moments later, Awa was broadcast ringing the opening bell on ten thousand square feet of Times Square's iconic LED screens. A videographer captured it all for Awa's inaugural post on Klik Klak.

The caption in the video read: *TFW you realize that the world finally sees you as the true badass you are.*

Next stop was over at The All-Stars Agency—TAA—the number one entertainment agency in the world. Talia was determined to sign Moussa and Awa with the best agent in the business, Steven Scotch. Steven had begun his career by launching megastars like Britney Spears, the Backstreet Boys, and Lady Gaga. Steven was not only the top earner at the agency, he was also a power broker—an entertainment lawyer who was known inside the industry as "The Hammer" because of his ability to nail the absolute best terms for his clients.

Steven invited the women into his corner office overlooking

Carnegie Hall. The walls were covered in platinum records, signed movie posters, and framed memorabilia. The room was a veritable museum of pop culture largess.

"Queen Awa," Steven said, leaning back in his chair, with a big smile and his hands in a pyramid, "you have been *everywhere* lately."

"Indeed." Awa winked at him. "The spotlight seems to follow me wherever I go."

"And you sparkle under its bright light."

Talia schooched forward in her seat and raised her Gucci-gloved finger, pointing at Awa and Steven. "I think the three of us will be... like... the most powerful trifecta in modern media, mkay. I'm thinking we should pitch a tell-all to one of the Big Five publishers, sign a Disney Plus deal, and create a swimwear line. Oh, and Awa's son is fabulous! King Moussa owns a surf and skate empire that we can really blow up from a retail and D2C POV and then sell... maybe to LVMH? So, what you're really getting with Awa is a two-fer, a two mermaids, one cup kinda thing. Royals, to boot! And, as if that's not enough, they're both gay, which is such a cool selling point. I mean... automatic cover of *Out* Magazine, right? Obviously we can't use Annie Leibovitz as the photographer... she has no idea how to light Black people. Did you see that Kamala Harris cover? Atrocious. OMG! What about getting Sir Steve McQueen to shoot them in a gorgeous interview and then seeing if he would want to go 2D for *Vogue*?"

Steven's eyes bugged out, his brain struggling to process the sheer volume of information Talia had blasted his way.

"I love it all," he replied, simply. "I can hear the angels ringing heaven's cash register. Soon enough, hundred-dollar bills will rain from the sky."

* * *

WHEN AWA and Talia stepped back onto the streets of Manhattan, FBI Agent Clark and her partner were waiting for Awa.

"Come with us," Clark demanded, opening the door to a government-issued black car. Awa waved goodbye to Talia and climbed inside. Once ensconced, Clark tore into Awa. "Is there anything you want to tell us about a covert mission you orchestrated in Greece?"

"What do you mean?" Awa feigned ignorance.

"We have received information from Bryce Dean that you attacked his mother and the whole of the Greek colony. Are you denying that?"

Awa shrugged. "Bryce is a notorious liar."

"Ms. Diop," Clark seethed, "the U.S. government does not take kindly to uncooperative allies. We need a better understanding of magical weapons, and if you are not prepared to share every detail of what you know, then you will be returned to your home country and barred re-entry here. And that's if we decide to be nice. If we decide *not* to be nice, we can declare you an enemy-combatant."

Enemy-combatant. Those words landed on Awa like a lead elephant dropped from the sky.

Clark's eyes burned. "Are you ready to talk now?"

19

May 5th

Gia and Shadow arrived in St. Moritz on a chilly morning. The last of the season's snow still clung to the town's famous Alpine crests. Gia checked into her hotel suite at Château Gelé and collapsed onto a fluffy sofa with a view of the hillside.

Shadow checked around the room, inspecting it and setting up the guards. "I would have preferred for you to stay at your chalet instead of this hotel. It is more difficult to track the comings and goings in a hotel."

Gia shrugged. "I need the cash flow from the rental of my chalet."

"I understand," Shadow said, nodding. "I'll stay a few more days to make sure you're settled and then get back to me usual penny-come-quick."

Gia eyed him, lips scrunched. "Queen's English, please." Although she did not understand Shadow most of the time, Gia had to admit that he entertained her.

"Ah, lady, you're breakin' me heart. All I mean is that I'll be back to cracking skulls for ya."

"I see." She offered him a satisfied smile.

"They'll be three men with you, always. I have 'em work in staggered shifts, so two of 'em always have eyes on you," Shadow explained.

"I do appreciate your careful planning and consideration, Shadow... but I am also much in need of privacy after spending ten days locked in a bunker with you."

"I don't mean it literal, Gia. They'll be around, and they'll take orders from both of us. You can have your privacy, but it's my job to keep you protected. So if they cramp your style for a few more weeks, that ain't a bad price to pay for safety."

"*Bene*," she conceded. "Anyway, with both queens gone, I feel much better. Moussa told me that Yiannis escaped. Apparently, he contacted Prince Kyle after the attack. But he is now in hiding."

"Oh, I'll find the bugger."

"I have no doubt. You are quite capable."

20

Thanksgiving 1996

There is nothing more depressing than being in a hospital during a festive holiday. Florent knew this from experience, because the year that he turned ten, his mother was hospitalized with encephalitis. On Christmas Eve, his father, Pierre, took him to the hospital to see her. Florent climbed into her bed to snuggle. There were no presents that year, only tears. Thankfully, his mother recovered by Valentine's Day, but Florent would never forget that lost, lonely Christmas. Maybe that was why he flinched when Diana suggested to Yia Yia that the three of them share a Thanksgiving dinner in Athena's hospital room.

In the late afternoon, Yia Yia arrived at Athena's room with a tower of overstuffed tupperware containers, filled with turkey and all the fixings, along with some special Greek additions to the traditional menu. Diana handed Florent a paper plate, and they all munched together in a semicircle with their eyes fixed on Athena. Yia Yia even prepared a plate for Athena, leaving it next to her head, hoping that the delicious smell might rouse her from her coma.

This is too much, Florent thought. *I should return to France soon and leave these women alone. I need to move on with my life.*

Just as they cut into the pumpkin pie and the baklava, Athena's heart rate monitor sounded an alarm. They bolted out of their seats and rushed to Athena's side.

Yia Yia panicked, asking Diana in sign language, "What's happening?"

"I don't know!" Diana yelled back.

A nurse ran into the room to check the machine and monitor Athena's vitals manually. She pressed a button on the wall and started screaming at Florent, Diana, and Yia Yia, "Everyone out of the room, NOW!"

Diana's face went white, and she begged the nurse, "Tell m—"

"GO!" the nurse commanded. Then she smashed the button on the wall again and shrieked into the loudspeaker. "CODE BLUE! ROOM 1409!"

* * *

Diana held back tears as she approached the nurse's desk again. "It's already been over twenty minutes. Can we go back in with Athena now?"

The nurse peered over her readers at Diana. "No, ma'am, you cannot. I've told you three times already. Please have a seat in the waiting room, and the doctor will be with you as soon as possible. All right?"

Diana balled up her fist and opened her mouth to say something nasty, but then thought better of it and walked away. She dropped herself into a chair next to Florent. Yia Yia signed furiously, trying to gather details, but Diana replied that she had nothing new to share.

"It's my birthday tomorrow," Florent whispered.

"Really?" Diana said. "You never mentioned anything about it."

"I almost forgot. My mother sent a card from France. It arrived in the mail yesterday."

Diana frowned. "I wish you'd told me. We could have gotten you a cake... or at least a cupcake... something. You've been so wonderful to have around. You know that, don't you, Florent? My mother and I are so grateful for all your support. There's nothing like having a man around. You've spoiled us." She reached out and squeezed his hand.

They heard footsteps coming down the hall, and they gazed up. The doctor beelined toward Diana. Florent tried to get a read on the man's face, but it was inscrutable.

"Mrs. Papadonis?" he asked.

"That's me." Diana started to rise, but the doctor waved his hands at her.

"No need to get up, Mrs. Papadonis. In fact, it's better if you sit." He bent down, crouching in front of her chair, so that they were at eye level. "I'm so sorry. I don't have good news for you. Your daughter went into cardiac arrest. That's why the nurse asked you to leave. We performed three rounds of CPR and also tried to resuscitate her with a defibrillator, but we were unsuccessful in restoring a heartbeat."

Florent felt his stomach drop.

Diana stared at the doctor blankly. "But... she's going to be fine, right?"

The doctor glanced briefly at Florent before returning his eyes to Diana.

"That's what I'm trying to explain to you, Mrs. Papadonis. Unfortunately, your daughter is deceased. We could not restore her heartbeat. She did not survive."

Yia Yia, who had been reading the doctor's lips, suddenly realized what the doctor meant. She doubled over in pain, sobbing. Florent reached out and consoled her.

"No," Diana insisted, "that's not possible. You're wrong. She still had a heartbeat when we left the room. I saw it on the machine."

"I'm very sorry for your loss." The doctor stood up. "Someone will come by in a moment to take you to see your daughter."

"Wait!" Diana shot out of her chair. "She can't be gone. She can't. I saw a heartbeat."

"I assure you, Mrs. Papadonis, we did everything we could."

"Why didn't anyone tell me she was dying?"

"My apologies. Our protocol is to focus on the patient and do everything we can to save their life."

"No, I mean... *today*. Why didn't anyone tell me *today* that she was dying? It can't happen from one second to the next. Can it? No one prepared me for this! I didn't even get to say goodbye!"

"I'm so sorry, Mrs. Papadonis. I don't have more information at this time. Someone will be by very soon. Please wait here." His white coat fluttered as he spun around and left the waiting room. Diana teetered in place, like the last pin in a bowling lane, struck by the ball but fighting to stay upright. She swayed too far to the left and lost her balance. Before she could fall, Florent was there to catch her.

When he got her settled into her seat again, Diana squinted her eyes at Florent. "We need to get you a slice of birthday cake."

He shook his head, no. "Don't worry about me, Diana."

"That's what Athena would want." Diana turned her head away as her tears spilled onto her cheeks.

* * *

FLORENT WAS the last of them to say his goodbyes. The truth was that he didn't want to see Athena's dead body. In fact, he rather wished he'd left weeks ago and avoided the morbid scene entirely. He seriously considered making a run for it, but Diana and Yia Yia were standing outside Athena's room, crying, and there was no way he could escape without passing by them. So, he took a deep breath and dipped his toe into the dead people pool once again.

He got a prickly feeling on his neck when he saw Athena in her bed. The sheet was pulled halfway up.

How strange, he thought. *Athena looks like she's sleeping. No... that's not true. It's like someone made a wax figure of Athena and carved it to appear as though she's asleep. Why do dead people never look like themselves?*

He hung back at first. He wasn't sure what he was meant to do. He'd seen people in the movies talk to dead people. He remembered Whoopie Goldberg in *Ghost*. He saw the movie with his mom in the cinema around the corner from his house. Whoopie had made him laugh so much. He could almost laugh now, thinking of the scene when Whoopie refused to hand over the check to the nun.

But laughing now would be wrong. I'll just say something to her... something short.

"Um... hello? *Bonsoir*, Athena. Happy Thanksgiving."

He paused, out of habit, which made him feel really stupid.

What am I thinking? She's dead, of course she won't talk back.

"I am very sorry that this happened to you." He shivered, because a wave of emotion was sweeping over him, and he didn't know what was coming his way, but it was very intense, whatever it was.

"I wish we had spent more time together. You were so beautiful... so kind. I love you, Athena." His next words got caught in his throat, and he freaked out.

Am I losing my voice again? Please, God... no!

He panted and mumbled some guttural noises, and once he assured himself that his voice wasn't disappearing, he continued.

"I found a photo of your father with... um... Marina Acquaviva. I never told you about Gia—but that doesn't matter now. And that's probably for the best. But Athena, I can promise you one thing... I will find out what happened to your father. I *will*. I think I have a good idea already. I believe Marina Acquaviva killed him."

21

May 7th

Riley handed Gia a glass of Kentucky bourbon on the rocks and then eased into the hotel suite's outdoor jacuzzi next to her.

"Damn," Riley said, "this view is stunning. All of St. Moritz is at our feet. Blessed not stressed vibes, huh?"

Gia blew Riley a kiss and then started in on her drink.

Riley turned slightly in her seat and peered through the window, observing the two beefy dudes inside. "Are these bodyguards a permanent fixture from now on?" she inquired.

"Why are you asking, Riley?"

Riley took a big gulp of her vodka soda and then replied, "It's pretty hard to *have fun* when someone is monitoring you all the time."

"I am sure they are very unconcerned about our sex life, *amore*."

"That's not what I mean, Gia."

"Then say what you mean, Riley. I am in no mood for mind reading this evening."

"Grrr," Riley growled. "Someone's in a sour state today. What's got a bee in your bonnet?"

Gia shook her head in frustration. "I have problems with the government in Macao. The authorities are demanding additional payments on my land lease for the casino. It is legalized extortion, pure and simple."

"The good news is that you have your Florent stash now, so at least you have money to pay them, right? By the way, how is that *fuckboy*?"

"Do not call him that," Gia snapped.

"Fuckboy?" Riley snorted, her tone souring.

"Riley, stop."

"But he *is* a fuckboy. Why are you defending him?"

"The man just saved my child from being kidnapped. He deserves respect."

Riley blinked a few times, like she'd been punched hard in the face. "Wow, Gia. Not too long ago you told me you were afraid of him and that you hated how possessive he is. Now you're singing his praises? Sorry, but you sound like an abused wife."

"We have a complicated relationship."

"Then I guess killing him is one hundred percent off the table?" Riley winced, hoping very much that Gia would give her the green light for murder.

"*Abbastanza!* Enough!" Gia smacked the surface of the water with her hand. "I told you already that Florent cannot be a target. Furthermore, I have too much going on at the moment, Riley. My focus is on myself, my child, and my business. The end!"

"Interesting." Riley stared down at her drink. "It's good to know that I don't factor into your list of priorities."

"How can you say this?" Gia fussed. "If you were not a priority, I would not be spending my time with you as I am now."

"Then what are we doing exactly? What am I to you? I feel like you're so distant these days. Half the time you don't even pick up my calls. It feels really shitty, you know?"

Gia paddled over and held Riley's head with both hands, kissing her hard on the lips. "You are special to me."

"I'm special? Gee, thanks."

"Stop pouting, Riley. I know you get very aroused every time you think about violence. I am the same. I understand you. There will be plenty of time to get into trouble together. I want to show you every-thing I know, but now is not the time, *amore*. Please, can you have patience a little longer?"

Riley blew a raspberry and then grunted. "Ugh, fine."

22

May 10th

Harper floated into the OTN boardroom, carried along by a cloud of thunderous applause. The most recent quarterly earnings report had boasted record advertising revenue, and Harper deserved every single clap that was directed her way.

Marlee lauded Harper to the board. "This is a historic moment for Our Truth Network. Harper Langley's fresh blood from the younger generation has infused the network with energy and enthusiasm. I can't say that I agreed with Harper's vision at the start, but she has that old Langley tenacity... and no problem twisting arms. OTN has seen a massive spike in the eighteen to thirty-four age bracket. Harper staked her strategy on Millennials, and with her fresh programming and focus on pivoting away from the far-right, she has captured the attention of Gen Z as well. I don't think I have to tell you all that such a feat was unimaginable just one year ago. Without further ado, I give you Harper Langley, our CEO."

A standing ovation followed. One board member even cried. It's amazing how emotional high-net-worth individuals become over rising stock prices.

Harper stood tall and proud at the podium. This was the true pinnacle for her. In this moment, sacrificing her parents seemed worth it for the adulation alone.

Dad would have offed me, too, if push came to shove, Harper thought. *Jesus, he's probably proud of me for having the guts to take them out.*

Harper acknowledged the outpouring of love with a humble "thank you" before turning her attention to the H2 strategy deck she had prepared. So far, she had turned OTN around with the sheer force of her will, but going forward, she would need the board's buy-in if she wanted to stay in power.

"We beat Tucker Carlson's ratings!" Harper screamed. "Let's have a moment of silence for the GOP!" She paused for dramatic effect and then said, "I'm only kidding! But, doesn't it feel good to know that we can still pull in huge numbers without Ronnie Spade's 'Make America Best Again' spiel?"

She glanced around the room, eyeing the faces of the elites that she had won over in *her* way, and Harper's heart puffed up like a plastic pool float.

23

May 14th

Absence makes the heart grow fonder, and Gia had not seen Florent in three weeks, so his weekend visit to St. Moritz was most welcome.

Gia met Florent at the front door of the hotel suite, wearing nothing but a silk slip. She threw her arms around him. "I missed you, *amore!*"

He took a step back. "Have we met?" he joked. "I don't believe I have ever seen Gia Acquaviva so happy to see me."

She answered him with a passionate French kiss. He wanted to continue teasing her with witty banter, but it was too late. She'd already won him over. He held her close and dipped her backwards, gathering the hem of her slip in his hands and pulling it up to reveal her bare backside. They made it halfway to the bedroom before they collapsed on the floor, desperate for each other.

That afternoon, they made love as they had never before. Gia let Florent touch her everywhere—and for as long as he wanted. She roamed his body like a master mapmaker, inspecting and admiring every inch of him. She ran her finger across his scar, and he flinched.

"You still do not trust me?" Gia's voice was low and forlorn.

He focused his eyes on hers. "I need more time, Gia. You hurt me very badly."

She bit her lip and nodded. She almost felt sorry for what she'd done to him. *Almost.*

24

May 15th

Gia slept all night, snuggled into the crook of Florent's arm, but she did not dream of him. No, it was Cameron who was that evening's guest star in her subconscious adventures.

Cam sped Gia down a dark road in a sports car. The seatbelt strapped across her middle was stretched out by her pregnant belly.

"Babe!" Cameron whooped, turning up the rock music blaring from the speakers. "Let's have another baby!"

In the rearview mirror, their eyes met. His were smiling, but hers were full of fear. Then, in the mirror, she spotted her parents in the backseat of the car. Marina's strawberry blonde hair whipped about in the breeze from the open window. Gia's father, Luca, wrapped his hands over Gia's shoulders and squeezed her. She laid her palm on her round belly and felt Serena flopping inside.

"She is kicking, Cam!"

Gia felt a sense of total comfort knowing her whole family was intact. She breathed a satisfied sigh and smiled to herself.

But when she turned her head back in Cam's direction, she saw that blood was rushing from a huge gash in his neck. He made fizzy, gurgling sounds and his hands flew off the wheel. He wrapped them around his neck, trying to stop the bleeding. The car veered to the right and was thrust onto its side. The impact from slamming against the pavement sent everyone except for Gia careening from the car. She laid in a tangled mess of metal and broken glass, searching for movement in her belly, wondering if Serena was still alive.

Suddenly, Gia's seatbelt unbuckled, and her father lifted her up into his arms, carrying her away from the mangled car.

"It was an accident," Luca explained. "You did not mean to kill Cameron. Your mother wants you to know that she understands this is all her fault."

"*Mamma!*" Gia howled. Suddenly, she was no longer on a dim, winding road in upstate New York with Cameron. She was fifteen and full of horror, bobbing on a boat in Monte Carlo, watching her mother battle with Adonis. The events unfolded as they had at that time: Adonis snarled his hands around her mother's neck with all of his might; Marina's face turned red; then Marina's sharp gills emerged, like the flap of a jet's wing; she sliced him clean across his throat.

His blood exploded onto her, onto everything, really. Then they fell together, his weight crashing her head hard against the wall of the boat. They laid in a limp heap like dirty laundry, their co-mingled blood lapped across the boat's deck. Gia shrieked as the wave of blood rushed under her father's shoes. She shook violently and wailed without stopping.

Her cries bled into the waking world, and Florent shook her awake. "Gia, you're having a nightmare. Wake up!"

She opened her eyes, still screaming and crying. Florent stroked her cheek and cooed to her. "Shhh. It's all right Gia. It was just a dream. Just a dream. You're here with me now, *chérie*."

It took nearly twenty minutes before she felt calm again. The whole time, Florent watched over her, kissing her every once in a while. He never asked her what the nightmare was about. He knew how closed off she could be about her feelings, and he felt it best that he not pry into her private fears. Besides, he understood better than anyone that she had done many things that would likely haunt her forever.

* * *

BY BRUNCH TIME, Gia was scrubbed up and decked out in a glamorous outfit. Florent and Gia linked arms and headed downstairs to the hotel's chic restaurant to meet Shadow.

Shadow greeted them in a small private dining room. The view showcased the town's snow-capped mountains and, in the distance, a shimmering lake surrounded by a piney forest. Immediately tensing, Gia stole a sideways glance at Florent. She would never forget that lake, and was sure Florent wouldn't either. He almost died there, so undoubtedly the vista brought back memories. She finally turned her head to meet Florent's gaze and searched his eyes for any emotion. He couldn't look at her. Instead, he kept his eyes trained on the lake.

Shadow noticed the tension. "Should we meet for dinner instead?" he asked, his eyes moving from Gia to Florent and back again.

"No," Florent replied, shaking himself out of his daze. "Of course not. Please, let's sit down."

"Gia," Shadow said, turning to face her, "I was hoping you would bring Serena with you. I got very attached to the babe when we were locked in the bunker."

Gia sipped her Bellini. "Ah, I left her in the careful hands of your hard men."

He guffawed. "Ain't that something? I have to pay them a visit after we eat. I need to see this for myself."

"I am feeling much more confident now that I know Queen Karen and Queen Zale are out of the picture. Not to mention my cousin, Yiannis. Good riddance."

Shadow flinched at her words and propped his elbows on the table, dropping his voice. "I have bad news, so I wanted to tell you in person."

"I do not like bad news," Gia snapped.

"Nobody does," Shadow answered firmly, "but it's bad news we got, so here it is. Yiannis is alive and sent a message to you through one of me men."

"*Fantastico.*" Gia gulped the rest of her drink and then slowly placed the empty glass on the table. "And what is it he wants?"

"He said he'll wave the white flag, but only if he can talk to you personally."

Florent jumped in. "That sounds like a bad idea to me."

"Risky," Shadow agreed.

Gia sneered, ignoring both men. "I certainly have many thoughts that I would like to say directly to his ratty little face. Set up the meeting."

Florent darted his eyes over at Shadow, and they exchanged a concerned glance.

* * *

AFTER FOUR GLASSES of champagne at brunch, Gia needed a jolt of energy, so she and Florent set out for a walk in the crisp air.

Florent spied the lake on the horizon. He steeled himself and then stated coolly, "We are going back to where it happened." He grabbed Gia's hand and marched her toward the lake.

When they reached the edge of the water, he turned to face her, every muscle tensed. He was waiting for her to break down or to open up... or generally to express some sense of regret, but she stood there with her mouth closed.

He looked away. "After the... um... after that night..." he felt his vocal chords contract reflexively. He cleared his throat and took a deep breath before continuing. "I didn't speak for many months after you slit my throat." His tone was pitchy and uneven. "Before that, I never realized how invisible the world makes you when you can't communicate in the *standard* way. If I had not been so full of rage, I probably would have killed myself."

Gia considered what he was saying; she heard every word, but she didn't understand what he wanted her to say in return.

"The *only* things that kept me going were unraveling the mysteries of your life and plotting my revenge. I was always there on the periphery, observing you. This I can say with confidence... I hate you."

Gia's face dropped. She started to speak, but he cut her off.

"I'm not finished," he hissed. "I hate what you did to me and to my father. I'm disgusted by you, but I also understand you, I think. More than anything, I feel sorry for you. You're pathetic. You prey on people's goodness. You scorn love in favor of... what? Thrills? You don't deserve to have the life you have. I wanted so much to rip it all away from you. I had planned for so long to come back into your life and then take everything you cared about from you. To crush you. I wanted you to feel small and insignificant, because that is how you made *me* feel."

His face was ruddy and hot, and the cold air made his nose a little runny, which, in turn, made him look like a young boy. Gia wanted to clean him up with a hankie. In his moment of pain, she found him precious and cute.

"I cannot go on like this anymore, Gia. Seeking revenge is like drinking poison, and I have felt sickness spreading into every part of my life for too long. I think you'll destroy me if I carry on like this. So, from today, I am choosing to forgive you. Do you hear me? *I forgive you*, Gia. Maybe that means nothing to you, because something is very wrong inside your beautiful head. You are probably convinced you did nothing wrong. But this is important to me... it's the most important thing I have ever done. I am letting go of my hatred for you, because... because I *love* you too much."

Gia gasped. "Ah... Florent... I—"

He stopped her talking by rushing over to her for a kiss.

Then he took her face in his palms. "Say nothing, Gia. I said what I said for myself. I am well aware that you will most likely make me regret it. For now, just kiss me and keep your thoughts to yourself. You're so good at that."

25

December 1996

Florent went into Macy's at Herald's Square. Actually, it would be more accurate to say that the mean winds of New York's winter *blew* him inside Macy's revolving door, because that's what happened. In the midst of the season's first massive blizzard, he had neither a proper coat, nor a suit to wear to Athena's funeral the following day. So, on that blustery afternoon, he sought both.

On the way to the men's section, he passed the cosmetic counters. A variety of perfumes wafted through the air like silk in a summer's breeze. He caught wind of a familiar scent: Gia's perfume.

Immediately, in his mind, he was back with her again, engulfed by her dark hair. Ensnared by her kisses. He could even hear her whispering to him, "*Amore.*"

He floated over to the counter, barely aware he was even walking. He picked up various bottles of perfume, trying to locate Gia's signature fragrance. Around the sixth or seventh, he found it. The bottle was a female bust, carved in glass.

The saleswoman greeted him with a big American smile. She

glanced down at his hand and noticed he wasn't wearing a wedding ring. "Shopping for your girlfriend?"

The question came at him like a freight train. He pictured Athena's face and felt overcome with sadness. It physically hurt for him to say, "No, I'm just browsing."

"All righty, let me know if I can show you anything. How about I give you a test strip? It's better to leave the perfume there for a moment, so you can let it settle and get a sense of how it really smells on the skin."

"I know how it smells," he snapped.

His sharp reaction jolted the clerk, and she retreated without another word.

He sprayed the perfume on his sleeve. Later, he bought a black suit and the most hideous winter coat imaginable.

* * *

ATHENA'S FUNERAL was humble and lightly attended; not because she wasn't well-loved, because she most certainly was. Rather, the small gathering was what Diana wanted. Diana couldn't face Athena's school friends and all of her acquaintances. Inside, Diana raged over losing her daughter before the girl's life had even begun. Therefore, Diana invited the minimum number of people that Yia Yia would allow.

Diana hid under a hat with a black veil. The veil served its purpose of creating a hard barrier between herself and anyone else. Behind the veil, she felt safe.

Because Diana chose to cremate Athena, the Greek Orthodox priest at her local church refused to do the funeral. Yia Yia hired a random Catholic priest recommended by the funeral home. The event felt slapped together, because it was. Diana had stalled in every way that she could. She didn't want to say goodbye to Athena.

After the ceremony, Diana hurried to the atrium of the mausoleum, hoping to get a moment to herself. She felt nauseated and hot. She lifted her veil and fanned her face.

"Diana?" Florent asked, walking up behind her. "Are you all right?"

She whipped around to face Florent. He was so young and handsome, and she thought back to the first time she'd met him at Tavern on the Green with Athena.

"Come," she replied, "give me a hug."

She rested her head on his shoulder and sobbed.

He patted her on her back and let her cry it out. After a few moments, she collected herself and dried her eyes and nose with several tissues.

"Florent, I know I have no right to ask you this... and please know that it's fine if you say no. I want to know... I... I would like for you to stay with me through Christmas. Do you think your mother could spare you? I don't know if I can face being on my own during the holidays. I might kill my mother."

Florent bobbed his head in reply. What else could he say to a grieving mother?

"Yes, Diana. I'll stay."

26

May 21st

Talia bent down and tugged at the hem of Queen Mother Awa's beaded cape, twisting it slightly to an angle, so that it would catch the light from the camera flashes on the red carpet.

"Fucking A!" Talia huffed. "Goddamn stylists. I shouldn't be the one down here fixing your outfit for photos. Ugh. Unless you're Nicole Fucking Kidman they triple book these days. So annoying. But you look great, Queen. A stunner! Now, smile!"

Talia stepped back and let Awa have her moment in the sun. Awa sashayed down the step-and-repeat, delighting the photographers with her dramatic poses and meme-able movements. Harper was waiting at the other end of the carpet, having served her time in front of the cameras only moments before.

"Harper!" Awa air-kissed her friend. "You look divine, darling. I've never seen you with your hair up. What a lovely neck you have."

"Thanks, it's an unwritten rule at OTN that blonde hair must always be down and flowing free at all times."

"Ha!" Awa clucked. "I don't know if you're aware of this, but you own the network now, Harper. I think you're allowed to sport a top-knot if you so choose."

The next celebrity made his way onto the red carpet, and the photographers went nuts, screaming. Ex-President Ronnie Spade smiled through his aging veneers. His infamous blonde wig was sprayed perfectly into place.

"RONNIE! OVER HERE!"

"HEY, RONNIE! SMILE FOR ME!"

"MR. PRESIDENT, LOOK THIS WAY!"

Harper scowled, took hold of Awa's arm, and pulled her away. "Shit, that's Ronnie Spade. Let's go. I don't want to run into him."

Awa's nose narrowed, and she visibly cringed, as if she had just smelled something rancid and rotting. "What is that old fool doing at a Climate Change gala?"

"Good God," Harper quipped, "he's doing what all fascists do. They hog the media spotlight and clog up the airwaves with their bullshit. And that turd is an absolute pro at just that."

"How did he even get invited? He's a Climate Change denier."

Harper rolled her eyes so hard she thought they might not roll back. "This is the problem with free speech... the Left thinks that to be 'moral' you have to give the other side a chance to express their views. But that just leads to more propaganda."

"My goodness, Harper," Awa chirped, "you sound like a true progressive. Don't let anyone hear you speak like that. The rednecks will snatch your network away from you."

Harper stuck her tongue out at Awa. "Haven't you heard? We've gone *politically agnostic*."

Awa lost it and exploded into laughter. "That's the funniest thing I have heard all y—"

"Well, well, well," a man's loud, nasally voice brayed behind Harper's back, "if it isn't Little Harper Langley all grown up."

Harper whipped around to see Ronnie Spade towering over her.

"Hello, President Spade," she replied evenly. "What a *surprise* to run into you here, of all places."

He frowned, and his jowls hung on his face like a droopy ball sack. "I don't like your tone, missy. You sound *nasty*." He turned his attention to Queen Awa. "And you... you're that *mermaid* woman that's always on TV now. You pull in good ratings, so I hear. I prefer our American born-and-bred mermaids myself. Corn-fed, so to speak."

Awa held out her hand for him to shake it. "*Enchantée, Monsieur le Président.* I am Queen Mother Awa Diop, formerly of Senegal. You may call me, Your Majesty."

He didn't take her hand to shake it. Instead, he muttered, "Formerly of Senegal? Hmmm." Then he sneered at Awa and whined, "Oh yeah, that's right. Our good ole' *American* mermaid Karen Dean smashed your little fish tank. That's too bad."

"Mr. President," Harper interrupted, "Queen Karen technically *isn't* American."

He puckered his mouth so that it looked like a clenched sphincter and then snapped, "I'll be sure to rectify that as soon as I'm re-elected." And with that, his Secret Service agents ushered him behind a curtain.

Awa felt a wave of nausea wash over her. "What an unpleasant troll," she whispered.

Harper's eyes widened. "Oh, you have *no idea*."

27

May 22nd

"...And then after Mr. Bisset's plane drops us off, we will arrive in Venice inside a delivery boat."

Gia listened intently as Shadow laid out the plans for the meeting with Yiannis, scheduled in two days' time.

Shadow unfolded a map of Venice, pointing as he explained each step. "We'll arrive at the casino first and establish a security perimeter. You and your arseface cousin will meet in the Eye, and then once you've said your piece, we'll take him away and deal with him."

"What about Serena?"

"I'll have two of me best men with her at your place."

Gia frowned as she considered this. "Would it be safer to keep her at Vittore's house?"

"Nah, nah. My boys are there now, setting up a new security system. It'll be a fortress."

"Make sure not to forget the trapdoor in the pool."

He tapped a finger against his head. "It's already right 'ere in this lump of lead. Everything's sorted."

"*Grazie*, Shadow."

* * *

LATER THAT AFTERNOON, Riley shuffled into Gia's suite, wearing a hoodie and oversized sunglasses.

"Are you hiding from paparazzi?" Gia asked, pleasantly bemused.

"Righteous hangover. It was mental last night. Jaysus, these super-hero actors can hold their liquor. I could barely keep up. Made a right fool of myself, I reckon."

Gia smirked. "Your accent is quite heavy today, Riley. I almost expect a kangaroo to knock on the door next."

"Awww," Riley cooed, smooshing Gia's cheeks between her hands. "I'm just the sad opening act for the Aussie petting zoo, is that it? Want me to wrangle a koala or two?"

The *au pair* entered the room with Serena, passing her to her mother. Gia held the baby on her lap, bouncing her.

"*Sirenetta mia, mia, mia,*" Gia babbled. "Can you say Mamma?"

Serena smiled at her mother and lifted her hand, pointing to Riley.

"That's Mamma's friend, Riley."

Riley feigned a smile and lifted her palm. "Um... hey... cute baby." Riley glanced up at Gia, grimacing. "Is Serena with us *all* afternoon?"

"Would that be a problem for you, Riley?" Gia asked, narrowing her eyes.

Riley scratched the back of her head. "No, no. Course not. Just... gah! Hangover, you know? Babies crying... hangovers... not a good combo." It was clear to Gia that Riley did not want to be around her child.

"I would like you to be able to spend time with me while I am with my daughter. I did not realize this was an issue for you. You have always known that I am a mother."

"Killer, you know I love that about you. I do... but maybe... today we can do a one on one and save the playdate for another time? Yeah?"

"Fine," Gia huffed. She stomped into the other room and dropped Serena off with the *au pair*.

When she returned, Riley was opening a bottle of wine.

Gia inspected the bottle and then plopped down on the other side of the kitchen counter. "You said you have a hangover."

"Hair of the Dog!" Riley winked and then poured Gia a glass.

"*Grazie*," Gia replied sharply, taking the glass from Riley. "I have been thinking, Riley..."

Riley winced. "Uh oh. I don't think I'm going to like where this is headed."

"Tomorrow I will leave for Venice for a few days. Perhaps we should take a short break."

"A break?" she scoffed. "We hardly see each other as it is. Are you... wait... are you *breaking up* with me?" Riley turned her head sideways and then eyed Gia like an angry crow.

"No, no. I have a lot on my mind, and I need to focus. I think it would be good to have some space."

"*Space* is code for breakup."

"Do not take this so seriously, *amore*."

"You know there's like a hundred million women out there who'd love to date me, right? I'm choosing to spend my time with you, and you're not treating me very well, Gia."

"Come here," Gia whispered. "I like you a lot, Riley."

Riley pouted and took her time getting close to Gia. "You do?"

"*Amore*, I want to see more of you, but right now, I need some time to take care of a few things. Is this all right?"

Riley pressed her lips against Gia's. "How can I say no to a femme fatale like you, huh?" Riley then bit Gia very hard on her bottom lip, drawing a little blood.

"Ow!" Gia snapped. "That hurt!"

"Meh." Riley scrunched her face. "You deserve it."

28

May 23rd

"Yiannis, are you really ready to die for what you believe in?" Queen Karen asked, her eyes burning with fury.

He replied with conviction, "I pledged my life to Queen Zale. She wanted Serena captured, and I intend to fulfill my promise to my queen."

"And where *is* your queen? They didn't dig her body up from the ruins, did they? She wasn't trapped like I was. So where is she? Is she hiding somewhere?" Queen Karen questioned Yiannis, and he squirmed.

"If Queen Zale were alive, believe me, she would be here now. I would be protecting her. Gia wants all of us dead."

"Gia does not know what she is up against," Karen quipped. A guard rolled her wheelchair away from Yiannis to give her a rest. She ached all over. Her body felt like a sack of broken bones. The attack on the Greek colony a month ago had not killed her, but it had maimed her badly and left her angrier than ever. She had been biding her time in Japan, eager to strike.

Now Gia—and more importantly, Gia's daughter—was within reach, just across the Croatian border in Italy.

Days ago, when Karen was still hiding in Tokyo, the Archivist had revealed something incredible to her. "We know that Serena can raise the dead," Togashi had explained. "It is also possible that she may be able to heal the injured. There is so much we do not know about her abilities. I need to examine her. She is the key to unlocking the secrets of Ancient Magic."

The possibility that Serena might repair Karen's crushed bones meant that she now had a personal motivation for kidnapping the baby and delivering her to Japan.

Getting her hands on the baby was Karen's only mission for tomorrow. With Yiannis and a small battalion by her side, she planned to succeed—no matter the cost.

* * *

AGENT CLARK MET Queen Awa in Washington Square Park, near a tuxedo-clad man pushing a baby grand piano on wheels. The musician sat at the edge of a fountain and began playing a Billy Joel song.

Agent Clark nodded to Awa and spoke first. "Thank you for coming all the way down to Manhattan to meet me."

"It did not seem optional," Awa snapped. "To be honest, you really put me on edge after threatening to make me an enemy-combatant. What is it that the United States needs from me today?"

"Bryce Dean has tipped us off that his mother is alive."

"Is that right?" Awa clucked. "So, Old Karen still has some juice in her. Interesting. What else did he say?"

"He mentioned that his mother intends to target Gia Acquaviva."

"Yes," Awa explained, "she seems rather single-minded about that."

"What's motivating her? Revenge? Wouldn't she be as concerned with retaliation against you?"

Awa's jaw tightened. She knew she couldn't keep the truth from Agent Clark and still expect to stay as a welcome guest in the States.

But it pained her greatly to be forced to reveal the information Gia had explicitly asked her to keep silent.

"The truth is that Queen Karen and Queen Zale are after Gia's daughter."

"Her daughter? Isn't she a baby? What would they want with a baby?"

"She's not just *any* baby, Agent Clark. She has magical gifts that the mermaids have not seen in a thousand years."

"What do you mean? What kind of magic powers?"

Awa winced. "She can reach beyond the world of the living... and... retrieve people."

"What!? Are you telling me that this *baby* is the human equivalent of *Pet Cemetery*?"

"I do not understand that reference."

Agent Clark moved closer to Awa and lowered her voice. "The baby brings people back from the dead?"

"Indeed."

"How do you know that, Queen Mother Awa?"

"Because she brought my son, Moussa, back to life after the tsunami."

Agent Clark's mouth dropped. Her mind spun as she thought about how government agencies might exploit such a power. The Mermaid world was proving to be even stranger and more powerful than she imagined. Plus, if she brought this breakthrough to her bosses, she might even get the promotion she'd been coveting for so long.

"I want to know everything about this baby," Clark whispered. "We might arrange some special perks if you could get me access to her."

29

May 24th

Gia, Shadow, and several teams of Shadow's hard men sailed into Venice before daybreak. Before they all disembarked, Shadow asked each team to sound off their location and mission instructions. He felt in control and at ease, because his troops were talented, well-paid, and experienced.

"And what about Queen Karen?" Gia asked. Awa had rung her an hour ago to pass on the unfortunate news that Karen was alive and planning to come after Gia. Granted, Gia felt less afraid since Queen Zale was no longer around to amplify the spell casting.

Shadow patted Gia on the shoulder. "Rest easy. Some of these geezers are Navy SEALs, Gia. They are trained in underwater combat. And we have scuba equipment standing by. I didn't want me men taking any chances when dealing with a merman like Yiannis."

Gia hugged Serena close to her, kissing her forehead. "Please keep my baby safe."

"I will guard her with my life," Shadow assured Gia.

A few moments later, he hand-delivered Gia to her safe perch within the Eye of her casino and then took off with Serena toward Cannareggio, to Gia's house.

Thanks to Gia's network of security cameras around the casino, she could see every angle of the establishment. Moreover, since Shadow's men were guarding all paths that led in her direction, she would know that Yiannis had arrived long before he ever set foot in the vicinity. The only thing she worried about was whether Queen Karen might still be alive and tagging along with him. What might the old sea witch do to Gia?

Gia put the thought out of her mind. As she waited for the day's events to unfold, her thoughts wandered through the past. She mused about the days when her parents were alive and running the casino. Gia remembered finishing school and racing to see her parents at the casino. After-hours, her mother let her play on the slot machines. Gia loved the spinning wheels covered in illustrations of brightly colored fruit and the loud metallic smacking of coins piling one on top of the other.

After her mother died, and then, less than a year later, her father, the casino became the center of Gia's life. Her grandmother Francesca took over management in an official capacity, but in reality it was Gia running the show, with a little help from Vittore.

Gia grew up instantly. There was no longer any time for childish pursuits. At sixteen, she inherited a vast fortune and became the de facto CEO of a complex business empire. She was forced to learn about things like money laundering and sex trafficking, to ensure that her casinos did not fall prey to such schemes. It was not an easy life to lead. The business required hard work and dedication and, most of all, time. As a result, she didn't form attachments to anyone her own age. The isolation only fed her rage. And by the time she was eighteen, she had become something of a monster, a shrewd businesswoman and a hungry predator, desperate to spill the blood of powerful men.

As she grew the portfolio and added clubs and bars to her holdings, Gia needed people she could trust to help her run the multinational operation. Her favorite cousin, Yiannis, was an obvious choice.

He had excelled in school and was known within the Greek colony as an industrious leader, an intelligent and resourceful thinker. She sat down with him once he turned eighteen and shared her vision for the business. He had wonderful ideas and was ambitious. Over the years, they built a strong relationship, becoming business partners in a sense. Therefore, Yianni's betrayal wasn't merely a professional one, it was deeply personal. Gia's self-worth had become so intertwined with her work that his betrayal cut into the very fabric of her soul, her identity.

So that day, as she sat at the helm of her business enterprise, on the very soil where it all began, Gia seethed with righteous indignation at her cousin's callous and self-serving behavior. After Kostas ratted her out, Gia thought she had seen the last of the attacks from her own family. She had no idea how very wrong she was.

* * *

IN THE LATE MORNING, Yiannis set sail toward a perilous confrontation with Gia. As the boat carrying him neared the Venice coastline, Queen Karen had her attendant steer her wheelchair into the water. She hung back in the lagoon with her battalion of Greek and Kiwi soldiers.

She closed her eyes and began to chant. The incantation would have been much easier with Queen Zale's enormous powers, but Karen had no choice other than to go it alone. Though her bones screamed with pain, Karen danced under the water, weaving a complicated spell to raise the tides.

* * *

AT FIRST, the change in the current was imperceptible. As a boat ferried Yiannis down the Grand Canal toward Gia's casino, it lurched forward, rocked by the increasing speed of the water below. By the time he docked, the water levels all over the city had risen slightly.

Yiannis was met at the door to the casino by two tall, imposing fellows. They took him by the arms, escorting him to the Eye. The guards searched his body for weapons, finding nothing. Then they deposited him across from Gia.

He nodded hello. "*Koúklaki mou,* it is good to see you."

"Do not lie," Gia hissed, "and do not call me your little doll. You make me sick."

"That feeling, Cousin, is mutual."

"How dare you, Yiannis! After everything I have done for you! How could you turn your back on me and *steal* from me? *Plot* against me? Threaten my life and the life of my daughter?"

"I serve one mistress, Gia. Queen Zale."

"Zale is dead, you idiot."

"Even so, everything I did, I did with a clear conscience. Gia, your thirst for power and your appetite for destruction... they are corrupting forces. You have caused irreparable damage to our people, to our way of life. Mermaids lived in peace for a thousand years until you disturbed everything. You have blood on your hands, Cousin."

"*I* have blood on *my* hands? Are you really so obtuse that you cannot see it is Zale who has caused the destruction? I never laid a hand on any merfolk. *Your* queen murdered hundreds of innocents... killed children, even! I may have brought unwanted attention to the colony, but Zale acted of her own accord in perpetrating horrors that will ripple through generations. She is a true beast."

"The queen did what she did to protect our way of life."

Gia scoffed. "You are nothing but a mindless zealot, Yiannis. You disappoint me."

"Likewise, Gia."

Their insults hung in the air as they scowled at one another.

But then Gia heard commotion on the casino floor. Water was seeping in through the doors, flooding everything. The staff and clientele attempted to rush out the front entrance or to take cover on the top of the card tables.

Gia watched everything on the security screens inside the Eye. Water rushed in from everywhere, so much so that it felt like the casino might float away.

"What is happening?" Gia asked the guards. "It is May... *acqua alta* only comes in the fall and winter. Has a pipe burst or is it something else?"

Yiannis grinned. "I see Queen Karen has arrived."

30

December 1996

About a week after Athena's funeral, Diana returned to work. She had to take her mind off of her grief, because at home there were constant reminders of Athena, and thinking of her daughter all the time felt to Diana like picking a fresh scab—until she bled to death.

Since Florent finally had his voice back, he decided that it would be a good time to check in with Leo, his detective in Venice. After all, he hadn't even told Leo that he had uncovered the first concrete proof that Marina Acquaviva knew Adonis.

They started off the call, talking briefly about everything that had happened to Florent since they'd last seen one another. Leo asked a lot of questions and was a wonderful listener. Admittedly, it felt good to speak to someone other than Diana and Yia Yia about his present circumstances.

"What a thing to happen to a young man," Leo said, upon hearing about Athena's passing. "You should get yourself a charm to guard against *Malocchio*. I am not a superstitious man, but you, kid, have run into a lot of bad luck, and I think you should protect yourself. Especially if you are set on continuing to follow Gia. She is evil incarnate."

Florent explained to Leo how he had found the photo of Marina and Adonis in Santorini.

Afterward, Florent asked, "Did you check birth records in Santorini?"

"We checked in Santorini, in Athens, in Thessaloniki... everywhere. I examined inside every donkey's asshole from the top of Greece to the bottom, and I am telling you, there is no record of Marina Acquaviva anywhere. It is as if she emerged from a clamshell fully grown, like Venus. By the way, did you ever find out what evidence the staff found in Suite 511 at the Hôtel Hermitage? That mystery has been nagging me for months."

"I haven't forgotten about it, but as you can imagine, there has not been a good time to bring it up with Athena's mother. I always wanted to ask Athena, but I never had the chance. I am staying with Diana, so I will find out somehow. Tell me, do you have any updates on Gia? Where is she these days?"

Silence followed, and Leo did not answer for an uncomfortably long time.

"Are you still there, Leo?"

"I did not want to tell you this, Florent. Gia is in New York."

"Where?"

"The Plaza Orientale... with her new lover."

Florent's heart ached, and it knocked inside his chest like a hungry guard dog locked in a cage.

"Who is it this time? A race car driver? A CEO? An obscenely rich old man?"

"Ah... a woman, actually. A Swedish politician."

Florent gnawed on the inside of his cheek. "I see. Thank you for keeping your eyes on her. Please continue to do so."

* * *

WHEN DIANA RETURNED from work that evening, Florent suggested that they go out. "I think a night out in Manhattan will do wonders for you," he cooed to Diana.

She sighed deeply, feeling that she might burst into tears. "It really is the last thing in the world I want to do, Florent." She looked at his face, so fresh and handsome, with eyes that were full of life, and she felt guilty. "You poor thing. You've been cooped up here with an old lady for too long."

"You are *not* an old lady," he insisted. "Put on a nice dress and let me take you for drinks."

A few hours later, they were ensconced in a booth overlooking Central Park and Columbus Circle.

Diana lit one of her candy-colored Nat Sherman's. "You're funny, Florent. The Plaza Orientale is not exactly the place I would imagine a man of your age wanting to frequent."

"Should I be blamed for my exceptional taste?"

"Ha, that's a good one." Diana raised her hand and asked for another round of martinis. "If it's all right with you, I plan to get good and sauced tonight."

"As you should," Florent concurred.

He had purposefully seated Diana facing the window, both so that she would be preoccupied by the vista, and also to block anyone else in the lounge from seeing him. While he was quite convincing at participating in conversation, Florent's mind was focused only on Gia. He surveilled the entire room, hoping for a glimpse of her long, dark mane.

Diana downed her third martini and nibbled on the cocktail onion and a side of olives she'd requested.

"Youuuu know what," Diana slurred her words, "you remind me of Adonis. I never realized until tonight. Same devilish look in your eye."

Florent flashed a smile and then sipped his drink.

"Florent, what do you plan to do when you return to France? Will you go back to school?"

He offered a small shrug as he contemplated this possibility. "I don't know."

Diana tisked. "It's not good for someone your age to be aimless. Especially after everything you've been through."

"I'm not aimless," he snapped.

Diana started on her fourth drink. "Sorry, I didn't mean it like that."

Florent tried to shake off her accusation. "My father was an entrepreneur. I would like to run my own company someday."

"Doing what?"

"Maybe something like what you do."

"Oh, my very glamorous work?" she teased. "Shipping and logistics... the perfect conversation starter to make any dinner guest fall immediately asleep."

"You are quite harsh to yourself, Diana. Do you realize that? You're accomplished and beautiful. Your life should not stop just because Athena and Adonis are gone."

Diana looked at him through unfocused eyes, "You don't know anything, Florent. You're just a kid."

Her words stung, but he was determined to make his point. "You are shrewd. Why do you think that you were able to take control of the company even though Adonis's whole family and his two ex-wives were after it?"

"Did Athena tell you that?"

He thought about his conversation with Leo earlier in the evening —and all the burning questions he had about Adonis. He was feeling liquid courage hit his veins, and he made a split-second decision to be bold and tell the truth.

"No. I have a private investigator. I had been seeking answers about someone else... and much to my surprise, the path led me to Adonis."

Diana tried to put the pieces together, but it wasn't making sense. She suddenly worried that she didn't know Florent at all, and maybe she had read him wrong. "What are you talking about? Did you hire this P.I. to get information about Athena's inheritance?"

"No, of course not! I was trying to get information about another person."

"Who?" Diana growled.

"It is not your concern."

"You better tell me this instant, or I swear I will... I will... I don't know what I'll do, but you will very much regret it."

He didn't realize until that moment how much he actually *wanted* to tell her about Gia. He'd been suffering for so long on his own, and now, here in front of him, was someone who was going through unimaginable pain just as he was.

"The person who did *this* to me." He tugged down his turtleneck, baring his scar.

"You said it was a skiing accident!"

"It wasn't."

Diana's face twisted in confusion and anger. "Who attacked you and hurt you?"

"I doubt you know her," he whispered. "But you may know her mother. Are you familiar with... *Marina Acquaviva*?"

Diana gasped and her martini glass fell from her hand, shattering on the floor in a thousand pieces.

31

May 24th

G ia burst out the doors of the Eye, shouting back at the guards. "Take Yiannis somewhere and keep him alive until I come back!"

She whipped through the flooded casino floor with great haste, her tail flapping wildly behind her. At the casino's exit, she was met by another set of Shadow's men. The water was already shoulder-high, and the men had to tread water to stay in place.

She blew past them and yelled, "Try to follow me, if you can!" She rounded a corner into a smaller canal against a strong current. The guards did their best to keep up, but they could not match her strength.

A short wall of water crashed over a bridge, washing it out. Debris hit one man, and he floated away. Gia zipped through Venice, taking every underwater shortcut to reach her *palazzo* as quickly as possible. She looked over her shoulder to see if Shadow's man was still following her, but he was long gone.

Citizens and tourists trapped in their houses and hotels screamed for help from the windows. Everyone was wholly unprepared for this strange, sudden flood. The police and coast guard weren't any help, either. Boats could not navigate the angry waters flowing through the canals.

As the water covered everything in sight, furniture, people, artwork, and centuries-old structures tumbled away in the current. Gia had never seen anything like this. Was Queen Karen really capable of all of this destruction on her own?

Gia said a silent prayer, immensely grateful that Vittore was safe in faraway Greece and not drowning in his barber shop down the street. Then her thoughts turned to Serena.

I have to get to my baby. I should have kept her with me. Why did I have to confront Yiannis? How stupid of me. I should have listened to Shadow and Florent.

As she turned to the left and approached her street, she darted to the surface. A row of merfolk—soldiers—were at her front door. They banged on it, but Shadow had reinforced it, and it wouldn't budge.

Suddenly, there were loud pops in the air, like fireworks exploding. A bullet knocked one soldier down. Then another. Blood spilled into the water.

All the time, the water was rising.

The soldiers split away, retreating until the water rose enough for them to swim over Gia's walls and into the courtyard of her palazzo.

When they were out of eyesight, she dove to the bottom of the canal and moved with careful strokes until she reached the secret hatch in her pool. She entered the code into the new security system Shadow had installed, and the door rolled open. She swam inside, into the bottom of her pool, and quickly closed the hatch door behind her.

She shot up to the surface. Water had flooded everything, but Shadow's men had strapped on their scuba equipment. They were armed with harpoons and ready to fight.

"Where is Shadow?!" she howled. "Where is my baby?!"

"He took your girl and dove into the pool as soon as the flood came in."

Tears welled up in her eyes and her chest tightened. "*Merda!*"

Another of Shadow's men jetted toward her, thrusting a spear gun into her arms. "Fight with us, Ms. Acquaviva!"

"I do not know how to use this!" she cried, nearly dropping the gun.

The guard helped lower the gun strap over her shoulder and showed her how to load the spears in. "Just hold the gun up like this." He hoisted her arms up to her eye level. "Aim by looking with both eyes through this little divot here." He pointed at a small ridge on the barrel of the gun. "Keep your eyes focused there and let the background go fuzzy. When your target's in sight, pull the trigger. I guarantee you'll hit it. Be confident!"

Gia's heart was pumping fast. Her tail thrashed in the water, keeping her in place. The men fastened their oxygen masks and scattered to their positions.

Water cascaded over the top of the walls, flooding everything. The battalion of soldiers splashed into the courtyard.

Shadow's sniper shot as many of the soldiers as he could until the tide washed him away. Then the hard men began firing their spearguns.

Soldiers screamed and charged the hard men, wrestling them underwater. One soldier used his gills and sliced clean through the throat of the man who had just given Gia instructions.

Then that soldier turned and beelined for Gia.

She held the gun as the man had explained. She talked herself through the directions in her mind.

Gun up, eyes focused, background blurry.

The soldier was in striking distance now.

Gun up, eyes focused, background blurry. Pull trigger!

She flexed her finger, and a spear landed between the merman's eyes, killing him instantly.

She pulled another spear from the pouch, trying to reload the gun, but it was tricky work and she dropped it. Blood swirled all around her, making it difficult to see who was coming at her. She trembled with fear.

Gia paddled backwards, taking cover inside her palazzo. The first floor was flooded up to the ceiling. She swam up the stairs. A soldier was right behind her. The soldier grabbed her tail, and she tried to kick him off. She succeeded, but he took a piece of her tail with him in his hand. She yelped in pain. A small trail of blood followed her. He lurched toward her again, grabbing her by the waist this time. She pulled a spear from the pouch and stabbed his hand. He winced and dropped back. She fled to her bedroom, trying to close the door behind her, but it was impossible underwater.

Her bedroom was completely submerged, and her bed floated in the middle of the room. It all looked like a dream or a surrealist photograph. She hid behind the mattress and reloaded the speargun. Her hands were shaking as she tried to hold the gun up to her eyes.

The soldier swatted at the mattress, sending it flying away, exposing Gia.

Gun up, eyes focused, background blurry. Pull trigger!

The spear shot through the water and punctured his stomach. He kept coming for her. She flitted toward the bathroom, zig-zagging to avoid obstacles in her way. Finally, Gia settled into the wall of the shower, using it to prop herself up while she reloaded the gun.

The soldier entered the bathroom. The gills in his arms were erect. He was aching to kill her.

Her hands fumbled while loading the spear into the gun.

He tried to reach for the gun and pull it away from her, but she struck the spear in his belly with her tail, which caused him to double over in pain.

She finally got the next spear loaded. She raised the gun and—

Wfffffppt! It sunk into his throat. He didn't survive the hit.

Gia had a moment to catch her breath.

The soldier's dead body floated in front of her. She finally had a chance to look at his face. It was a face she knew well.

She was staring at her grandfather, Triton.

32

May 24th

Gia abandoned her grandfather's dead body and escaped out the window of her palazzo in search of Shadow and Serena. She zipped through the canals, looking everywhere.

She turned onto a narrow path... one she had traversed so many times before. It brought her to the edge of the Hotel Bauman.

Suddenly, it hit her—Shadow must have taken Serena to the cavern below the hotel. Surely after years of working with Florent, Shadow would have known about Gia's hiding place. She dove down, down, down, into the crevice below the hotel, her eyes lighting the way.

How long could an oxygen tank possibly last? Gia wondered. She worried that Shadow might not be alive, if in fact he was down there at all.

In the distance, many meters below, she saw a halo of light. Her pulse quickened, and her tail flopped, propelling her down.

What she found when she arrived shocked her.

Indeed, Shadow had taken Serena to the cavern for safekeeping. He was holding the happy baby in his arms.

But what Gia never expected to see were Shadow's two glowing eyes staring back at hers, and his magnificent tail, silvery-grey and somewhat shiny, like pencil lead.

Shadow smiled wide and passed the baby to Gia, who then snuggled Serena close to her. Both mother and daughter were gently flicking their tails in the same rhythm.

Gia couldn't take her eyes off of Shadow.

In general, she hated surprises, but discovering that Shadow was a merman brought her great joy.

She had a million questions, but for now, she just held her baby and felt a warm wave of exhaustion pass over her.

* * *

WHEN GIA and Shadow finally emerged from the empty cave under the Hotel Bauman, they encountered a version of Venice that differed greatly from the one that they had sailed into that very morning. The flood had caused much of the beloved city to collapse into itself. First responders tended to the lucky people who had survived, because many had not. Corpses crawled through the canals like zombie children in a lazy river.

It was a gruesome scene, even for someone like Gia, who was used to being up close and personal with death. Furthermore, Venice was her hometown. Her heart ached to see it destroyed—and by her own family to top it off.

Her family. Her fucking traitorous family. How could her grandfather attack her as he had? Her stomach sank as she thought of him floating all alone in a watery grave.

Gia, Shadow, and Serena took off for the casino. There was still the matter of what to do with Yiannis.

* * *

SHADOW COLLECTED the remaining hard men who had survived the battle and swooped them up into Florent's cargo boat along with Gia and Serena. Yiannis was gagged and bound in the corner of the boat. Once they sailed out further into the Adriatic sea, away from the view of other boats, Shadow took Serena out onto the deck and left Gia with two guards.

It was time for Yiannis to face his punishment.

She ordered one guard to punch him in the stomach.

Yiannis grunted in pain, and Gia ripped off his gag, slapping him in the face.

She screamed at him in Greek. "*Figlio di puttana!* You are a motherfucker, Yianni. Do you know that I murdered my own grandfather to stay alive? That was one of the worst moments of my life!"

He didn't reply. What could he say? He didn't intend to beg for his life. The jig was up. He prayed only for a quick death.

But a quick death was not a blessing Gia afforded him.

The guards tied him up and hung him from the ceiling of the boat. She tortured him slowly, over hours, ripping into his skin with her gills, making sharp little cuts. She sliced him anywhere she fancied: his shoulders, the soles of his feet, between his legs.

He sobbed in pain, but never asked her to stop.

When she had finally had enough, she slit his throat and left him to bleed out like a slaughtered pig.

33

May 25th

Queen Mother Awa's heart fluttered as she buzzed Agents Clark and Sullivan through the gate of Langley Manor.

Mariama met the agents at the front door and showed them into the sitting room. Awa greeted them with a fresh pot of coffee.

Awa poured them each a cup. "Thank you for coming in the middle of the night," she said. "I wanted you to hear this from me first. Queen Karen and a group of soldiers attacked Gia in Venice. They have practically destroyed the city. The death toll is going to be very high."

Clark shot Sullivan a horrified glance.

"Gia survived," Awa explained.

"And the daughter?" Clark asked.

"She is unharmed."

Agent Clark breathed a sigh of relief. Just as she had imagined, her bosses were overjoyed about the prospects of that so-called miracle baby and eager to get their hands on her.

Clark stirred a sugar into her cup. "The U.S. government cannot allow this violence to continue unchecked. We have to intervene."

Awa pursed her lips. "What are you suggesting, exactly?"

Agent Sullivan offered a suggestion. "I think we need to bring all the parties together, along with President Bowden. Apparently, he has become increasingly concerned about Magical Weapons of Mass Destruction and the collateral damage of the Mermaid Civil War."

"*Magical Weapons of Mass Destruction?*" Awa sputtered. "What is that?"

"It's what the administration is calling the spell casting," Clark explained. "In the absence of a thorough understanding of the matter, the military has been making up their own lingo as they go."

"Isn't that wonderful?" Awa snapped, rolling her eyes.

Clark shrugged. "We're going to have to run this all the way up the chain to the very top. Can you organize a meeting with the leadership of each nation?"

Awa exhaled sharply. "I can try."

34

Christmas 1996

Fuzzy flakes of snow piled up on the windowpane in the guest bedroom in Diana's mansion. A light knock at the door awoke Florent.

"Come in," he called out.

Diana poked her head in. "Merry Christmas."

"*Joyeux Noël*," he replied, sleep in his voice.

"May I come in?"

He nodded.

"Thank you for being here with me, Florent. It means a lot to me not to have to be alone," she smiled. "I have a little something for you."

Florent threw back the covers on the bed. "I also bought you something, Diana. Wait here." He rose and took out a rectangular box wrapped in silver paper. "You go first."

She took her time opening the gift. As rich as she was, she still hated when people ripped good wrapping paper to shreds. She kept an entire closet full of discarded wrapping paper that she reused. In fact, Florent's little present was covered in re-gifted paper.

When she opened the box, she discovered that it contained a Jean Paul Gaultier perfume bottle in a silver can. It was Gia's perfume, but Diana didn't need to know that.

"How nice, Florent!" She took out the bottle and sprayed her neck.

Immediately, he was hit with the scent of bergamot, vanilla, and musk. He closed his eyes for a second and let his mind wander back to those first days in Paris with Gia. He often thought about the fun he'd had with Gia and Dimitri—he missed those days more than he liked to admit.

Diana interrupted his reverie when she asked, "Do I smell good?" She leaned forward and let Florent take a whiff.

"*Magnifique*. Delicious."

"Open yours." She pressed the box into the palm of his hand, and he immediately tore into the paper, much to her chagrin.

Inside the box was a greenish coin that looked ancient. And there was a weathered note, written in a different alphabet. Greek maybe?

He rolled the coin around in his palm. "What is this?"

"That, Florent, is what Marina Acquaviva left in the room she rented for Adonis at the Hôtel Hermitage."

"*Non!*" His eyes lit up. "You took this from Suite 511?"

"I sure did."

He picked up the note and passed it to Diana. "What does this say?"

"It says, 'Fuck off' in Greek."

"And you are sure it's from Marina?"

"It has to be. She was the only other person who was in that hotel suite, and the writing isn't Adonis's."

He inspected the coin and the note. "What does it mean?"

Marina sighed. "I wish I knew. It has been haunting me for years. I asked a coin expert about the gold, and he said it's ancient, likely from a shipwreck. That certainly makes sense, because Adonis was obsessed with diving and finding treasure at the bottom of the ocean. Silly, if you ask me. And the note... who knows? From the scene in the hotel, Marina attacked Adonis. It seems like she wanted revenge. I don't know for what... but..." Diana stared out the window, lost in her memories. "Sometimes Adonis was a real son of a bitch. Maybe she had her reasons to be angry. I only wish that I had the answers about what happened to him."

35

May 27th

They call it the "Top of the World." The glitterati come to St. Moritz for its famous ski slopes, but they stayed for the champagne climate. Home to mineral springs and abundant forests, the chic village also draws a summer crowd. Late spring brings heavy rain and wildflowers as far as the eye can see. Today, though, the sun awoke and claimed the day.

Gia rose from her slumber to find Florent making her an espresso. They had their coffee on the deck, soaking in all that Alpine glory. She finally felt relaxed again, knowing that she had taken care of Yiannis for good.

"The scenery reminds me of *The Sound of Music*," Florent mused.

"Oh?" Gia asked. "Will you run to the top of the mountain and serenade me like Julie Andrews?"

Florent chuckled. "You would like that, wouldn't you? Seeing me turn round and round in circles?"

"I am sure we can find you an apron somewhere. I would like the full experience, please."

He slid out of his chair and approached her, nuzzling her face with his prickly, unshaven skin.

She put both hands on his cheeks and kissed him.

"Mmm!" Florent smiled with a devilish grin. "I almost forgot, Gia! I have a surprise for you."

She grunted. "You know I hate surprises."

"Oh, but you will love this. I have organized a private yoga session... with baby goats!"

"Florent, stop. Do not tease me."

"I am quite serious, Gia! I thought you could bring the *au pair*... and Serena could pet those smelly little goats. My daughter loves all animals. Serena is probably the same."

Gia realized for the first time that Serena had never been around any animal. The baby didn't exactly have a *normal* start to her life.

"All right," Gia accepted, feeling amused by this new development on the itinerary. "I will shower and then... baby goats."

* * *

"THEY SMELL AWFUL, FLORENT!" Gia backed away from a small crowd of baby goats snacking on treats from Florent's hands.

Serena tugged on the horn of a black and white goat, babbling and smiling.

Florent took notice of the golden-haired babe. "But look how happy she is, Gia!"

Indeed, Gia had never seen her daughter this animated. Seeing the bliss in her daughter's eyes, Gia felt overcome.

To think I almost lost her again. What would have happened to her?

Nearly in tears, the only word that Gia could muster up without crying was, "*Bellissima!*"

She watched as Florent scooped up her daughter, sweeping her through the air. Serena squealed with delight.

Vittore is right, she thought. *I have another chance at love... at a family. It will be very difficult to give up Riley, but she is not ready for the life I have.*

"Are you all right, *chérie*?" Florent called out, turning his head in her direction. "You seem upset."

Gia offered Florent a small smile. "No, *amore*. I am so happy, truly." He mimicked her expression and went back to playing with Serena.

After yoga, the *au pair* played with Serena in the grass nearby, and Florent and Gia sat on a blanket, drinking white wine.

Florent sighed and tipped his face backward to feel the sunshine on his face. "*Merveilleux*. What a spectacular day."

Gia ran her hand along his leg. "It is the best day I can remember," she purred.

"Is that so?" He leaned over to kiss her, breathing a contented sigh.

Not since her first days with Cameron had Gia felt so free. Then again, Cam never completely knew who she really was. Florent knew all too well... and he loved her despite it.

Why does he love me so much? I do not deserve his affection.

He cozied up to her. "Put your head in my lap."

She laid on the blanket and rested the back of her head on his legs. He stroked her hair. She closed her eyes, enjoying the tingles in her scalp.

Is this genuine love? Is this what I have been missing?

Just then, the *au pair* squealed, "*Madame!* Look at Serena! She is walking!"

Florent and Gia sat up and saw that indeed, Serena was taking her first clumsy steps.

"Oh, Florent, should we help her?" Gia tugged on the edge of his shirt. "I do not want her to fall and hurt herself."

"She will be fine, *chérie*. The grass is very soft."

Florent took his eyes off Serena for a moment and met Gia's gaze. She smiled at him, and he felt his heart soar. He leaned over and kissed her, holding her head tenderly with both hands.

Gia glanced back over at Serena. "I worry about Serena sometimes," Gia confessed. "I worry that she will grow up to be like me. I do not want that. I want her to be good... to have an peaceful life and to be happy."

Florent sighed. "We all want that for our children. I have the same hopes and dreams for my daughter."

"Serena," Gia called out. "Come to Mamma!" She held out her hands, and Serena came bounding across the uneven ground, tripping and falling into Florent's lap. He gathered her up and kissed her on the forehead, passing her to Gia.

"She's beautiful, just like you are, Gia." He hugged both of them close to him and grinned.

"*Amore*," Gia whispered to him. "Thank you for today. It has been one of my most favorite days ever."

He chuckled and replied, "If you would let me, Gia, I would give you ten thousand days exactly like this. I love you so much, *chérie*."

Gia bit her lip. "I love you, too, Florent."

In his mind, he pictured himself living with Gia in Paris, creating a beautiful, blended family with their two daughters. The thought brought tears to his eyes. It was a wonderful dream, one he hoped very much to make a reality.

36

June 1st

The U.S. Consulate General's office in Rio de Janeiro had hosted its fair share of world leaders, but nothing like today's strange yet illustrious meeting. American President Jonah Bowden was set to arrive at two o'clock, but the Secret Service had been in the building since the day before, prepping security.

The leaders of the Atargatic nations arrived at staggered times, as was the request from the Consulate General. First came President João of the Brazilian colony. Next up were Queen Mother Awa and King Moussa, followed by the representatives from New Zealand, Hunu and Pania. The Arctic Circle sent only Skirlor to speak on behalf of the Ice Folk. Prince Kyle was a stand-in for his fugitive mother and locked-up brother. Representing the Japanese was Akiko. And the last leader to arrive was Prime Minister Rio Dulce of Belize. The Greek colony was in shambles and therefore sent no representative.

The Consulate General feted the motley crew and toasted them with a non-alcoholic punch, before announcing the arrival of President Bowden.

Jonah Bowden was a jovial man in his late 80s, the oldest U.S. president ever. He had a slight lisp because of his dentures. With a head full of white hair—thanks in part to a hair transplant during the 1990s—he looked like a handsome great-grandfather.

Queen Mother Awa reached out her hand first. "President Bowden, I am very pleased to meet you. You were always a favorite American politician among my people."

He smiled widely. "Wonderful to meet you, Your Majesty. Senegal is a beautiful country. I have been many times. I even went surfing once there with my grandson."

President Bowden then made the rounds in the room, greeting every leader and exchanging pleasantries. Before long, they took a seat at the large round table in the conference room.

The president kicked off the formal meeting by announcing his intentions. "Today I would like to discuss a path toward peace. The violence has to stop."

"Mr. President," Awa replied softly, "with all due respect, our hostility is not toward the U.S. government. I fervently hope that the Atargatic nations can settle our differences without outside influence."

Curious, Akiko turned her head. "And yet, Queen Mother Awa, you have been providing the U.S. government with information. You admitted it yourself. I saw it on television."

Awa balked. "I have been proactive in my relationship with the FBI. Is that a crime? I have spent months building trust, hoping that the U.S. would extend goodwill to all the Atargatic nations."

"Be clear," Akiko continued. "Your intentions have not been entirely as altruistic as you are suggesting, Your Majesty. On the contrary, you were hoping to receive favorable treatment and to increase your celebrity status in exchange for your cooperation. That is quite obvious."

"Woah now," President Bowden said, extending his hands, fluttering them. "Let's simmer down. America has no interest in playing favorites, okay? The fact of the matter is that the Mermaid Civil War is affecting humankind on a rather massive scale at this point." He sat back, threading his fingers together and collecting his thoughts. "The truth is that after the fiasco in Venice, people are outraged. Public sentiment has shifted, and the fascination with mermaids has turned into fear and rage."

The president turned his attention toward Kyle. "Prince Dean, I understand that your mother was the architect of the attack on Venice. What does Queen Karen say now about her plans... and her attitude toward peace?"

Kyle cringed. "Mr. President, my mother didn't dictate exact words to me... but what I can say is that she's not particularly *inclined* toward taking any path that doesn't give her exactly what she wants."

"That's too bad," President Bowden replied, leaning back in his chair. "In politics, no one gets exactly what they want. Your mother knows that."

"How right you are," Awa agreed. "All the same, I think we can agree that there are a few bad actors driving the conflict."

Prime Minister Rio Dulce leaned in. "Would you count *yourself* as one of those bad actors?"

"You must be joking, Prime Minister. Do I need to remind everyone that our colony was *completely destroyed,* and that we lost *seventy-five percent* of our people? I am appalled by the false equivalency being leveled against me today."

President Bowden cleared his throat. "Ahem. Could someone please enlighten me on the genesis of this conflict?"

Akiko glanced around the room and then spoke up. "As far as I understand it, all the Atargatic nations maintained peaceful relationships until Gia Acquaviva was excommunicated from the colony in Greece."

Kyle raised a finger. "And I want to point out that I voted in favor of that excommunication because Gia outed us to the World of Man. *Among other things.*"

Moussa kicked Kyle under the table, irritated by the fact that Kyle was throwing Gia—and his mother, by association—under the bus.

"So," President Bowden continued, "most of you view Gia Acquaviva as the aggressor? What has her role been in these attacks?"

Awa tapped a pen on the table. "Mmm. No. I'm not liking the direction of this conversation. Queen Zale and Queen Karen launched an unsanctioned act of war on my colony, resulting in *genocide*. Genocide!"

Prime Minister Rio Dulce was aghast. "Pardon me, Queen Mother Awa, but you turned around and did exactly the same thing in Greece. Albeit, you hid behind Skirlor and the Ice Folk. I suppose that since you do not have magical abilities, you saw fit to have others do your bidding. Did you know that the Greeks are still digging dead bodies up from beneath the rubble? Frankly, it is heartbreaking."

"I see," Awa scoffed. "So, it's heartbreaking when Greek people die, but when my people were slaughtered, you did not even care to take a stand and support us. Is that because we are Black? Do the same race-based hostilities that are a blight on the World of Man now plague our world as well?"

"I resent that!" the Prime Minister snapped. "I have always supported you. Do not dare call me a racist."

President Bowden frowned and intervened. "Let's table this portion of the discussion for a later time. There's another issue we need to discuss... which is Magical Weapons of Mass Destruction."

Skirlor eyed President Bowden with suspicion, but remained silent.

A Secret Service officer handed President Bowden a folder marked "Confidential: Clearance Required."

Bowden cracked it open and glanced at the papers inside. Then he said, "The Pentagon would like to initiate a task force to boost our understanding of Magical Weapons of Mass Destruction. I would like to invite three of you to join this task force."

No hands went up.

President Bowden sucked his teeth. "That is a real disappointment. Let me make something clear here. The United States government... and NATO and the U.N. for that matter... will not stand idly by as you... *people* destroy our cities and create mass carnage. Now, you either get with the program or you don't. We have the power to neutralize these kinds of threats. You all do not want to make an enemy of the U.S.A. I can assure you that."

He made firm eye contact with everyone in the room before asking again, "Do I have any volunteers for the Pentagon task force?"

Every hand went up except for Skirlor's.

37

September 2005

The relationship between Florent and Diana evolved slowly over time. After the first Christmas that they spent together, she invited him to come and work with her at the shipping company.

"You seem interested," she had said back then. "I'll teach you everything I know."

So, he became Diana's apprentice. He was intelligent, a quick learner. He took on more and more responsibility, which, little by little, brought them closer together.

It was nearly two years after Athena passed away before they ever even kissed. Florent liked who he was when he was with Diana. She always praised him and treated him with kindness and respect.

In 2001, they married at City Hall. Yia Yia was not in attendance, because they did not have her blessing. She found their union distasteful and disrespectful to Athena's memory. It was years before she spoke to them again.

Much had changed about Florent's life, but one thing remained forever constant: his focus on Gia. Sometimes he wondered why he couldn't just move on from her. Maybe it was because she had hurt him so much, cut him to the core. Maybe it was the mystery of Marina and Adonis. But more than likely, the true engine behind his obsession was his raging desire for revenge.

In the fall of 2005, Diana and Florent headed to Venice to close a deal on a shipyard. Carting goods into the floating city was big money, and Florent and Diana chased every dollar bill that fluttered into their sphere. After all, pennies make dollars, and dollars make millions.

He convinced Diana to stay at the Hotel Bauman, because he knew from Leo's intel that Gia was currently in town, and he also knew that the hotel was Gia's favorite stomping ground. Mysteriously, the Swedish politician that Gia had been with in New York had disappeared long ago, but that story was ancient history. Gia had a new fish on the hook these days, a hotshot lawyer from South Africa.

At night, Florent would sneak out of the room while Diana was sleeping. After Athena's death, Diana had become overly reliant on benzos to help her sleep. Florent often used those late nights to study Gia's movements throughout the world. He'd been clever enough to have Leo attach a tracking device to her newly acquired jet. With his experience in logistics, Florent could keep tabs on her at all times. And everything he learned about her went into a growing case file, held under lock and key for when the right time presented itself.

And Florent was patient, because he knew eventually it would.

Florent had asked Leo to help him patrol in the evenings for Gia. One night Florent caught sight of her and began following her. Being near her, mere steps away, made his pulse soar. The truth was that she was the most exciting thing in his life. He justified allowing her to murder innocent people, because he knew that one day he would deliver her comeuppance.

If he was lucky, tonight would be the first time he watched her in action. He was dying to know what she did with the bodies.

Gia was with the lawyer she had been dating. She led her lover down a dark alley and onto her riva. Florent followed. Gia kissed her love in the backseat of her boat, under the moonless, cloudy sky. The night was balmy. She unbuttoned her blouse and let her lover devour her breasts.

Florent observed everything from the shadows, safely hidden in a doorway. As he watched Gia undress her lover and climb on top of him, Florent found himself becoming very aroused. His face burned hot with shame as his cock grew harder.

What happened next went rather quickly. Gia's lover leaned his head back, groaning with intense pleasure. The boat rocked as Gia bounced on his lap. Then, the strangest thing happened. Gia lifted her right arm, and something emerged from under her skin. It was hard to see what, exactly. It certainly wasn't a knife. It looked like a gill. The man's eyes were closed, so he was none the wiser.

The blood rushing in Florent's ears was so loud that he was sure Gia might notice it at any second and whip around to meet his eyes.

But she didn't.

Instead, Gia brought her arm down with tremendous force and sliced at a diagonal, cutting the man's throat open. He tried to scream, but could not. Florent braced himself against the doorframe. His hand shot up to his own neck. He felt the lump of his scar running along the inside of his palm. He knew exactly the unbearable pain the poor man was feeling right now. Florent had to fight the urge to rush over to her, strangle her with his bare hands, and throw her into the canal. He was equally horrified, terrified, and angry.

Gia was enjoying herself. She even smiled. She held her lover's head back and watched him writhe for a long, long time. His blood gushed out, covering Gia, and she reached her fingers down and spread his blood on her clit. Florent gagged.

When the man was finally at peace, Gia shoved his lifeless body into the canal and disappeared with him under the water. A few seconds later, Florent witnessed something absolutely crazy. In fact, it was so insane that he wiped his eyes like some kind of cartoon character.

He saw a tail. A fishtail. More precisely, a *mermaid* tail, kicking through the current.

He followed behind her, tiptoeing over dilapidated bridges and winding pathways until they arrived at the Hotel Bauman. Then he lost her. He waited outside to see if she would come back, all the while wondering where she had gone and how long it was possible for her to stay underwater. An hour or so later, she finally appeared.

And the body was nowhere in sight.

There was only one explanation. She must have left her lover somewhere near the hotel. Where, Florent wasn't sure. But if she was a mermaid, then logic told him that the man was somewhere underwater. Probably alongside a great number of other lost souls.

Florent reached into his pocket and rubbed Adonis's gold coin with this thumb, contemplating what to do next.

38

June 3rd

Gia poured herself a drink and settled onto the sofa in her suite, crossing her legs. She beamed at Shadow, who sat next to her, drinking a fresh espresso she had made for him. "Shadow, before we start on the business of the day, you must tell me more about yourself. As you can imagine, I was shocked to discover your secret."

"And I hope that we can keep it between us."

"I would not dream of exposing you. I know better than anyone how damaging it can be when you are outed against your will. When my cousin Kostas told the world about me, I had never felt so unsafe and vulnerable. I will conceal the truth about your identity for as long as I live. But tell me... where do you come from... which colony?"

He covered up his mouth with his hand to obscure a huge grin. "Never told anyone this before. Feels strange to say it out loud. My nan was from Nigeria, and she fell in love with an English geezer. Turns out, he was a merman. See, there's a whole lot of us. My people's been living in the River Thames since..." he blew air out of his lips, "since the Dark Ages, probably. We're the descendants of Melusina."

"*Melusina?*" Gia laughed. "The freshwater goddess? My mother told me fairy tales about her. I always thought that she was a myth."

He shrugged. "Truth is stranger than fiction, eh? I grew up right near London Bridge. Now, how's that for a fairy tale?"

Gia gulped her drink. "I should call you my Charles Dickens."

"Ha!" He howled with laughter. "*Charles Dickens?* More like Oliver Twist!"

They both giggled.

His eyes sparkled, and then he said, "I'd like to take you home one day," but he caught himself and then added, "for work, of course. For work... uh... networking and such like."

Gia nodded, doing her best not to call him out and embarrass him.

"Shall we turn our attention to business?" she asked.

He winked at her. "Probably best."

She took his hand in hers. "*Allora*, first I want to thank you... sincerely and from the bottom of my heart, Shadow. You saved my daughter. I will be eternally grateful to you for that. I lost my parents when I was very young. It is now my worst fear that the same will happen to my baby."

"Ain't gonna let that come to pass." He was still squeezing her hand, and she felt her palm begin to sweat.

She dragged her hand back and stood up straight. "Regarding business, shall we begin with Macao?"

"My cow, my beautiful cow! All right, so the update from Macao is that my men have worked out your issues with taxes and the land lease. All is well. We need to stock the coffers and then we'll be back to makin' bees and honey."

"Money?" Gia said, scrunching up her nose.

Shadow gave her a thumbs-up. "Right you are."

"Regarding the cash-on-hand for Macao, Shadow..." Gia paused, wincing. "I cannot spare twenty million. Could we get by with ten to start?"

He thought for a moment before answering. "Hmmm. That will be tight, but I think I can make it work."

Gia breathed a sigh of relief. "I am so glad to have you on my team, Shadow. You cannot imagine. It was very hard for me to lose Yiannis. Nothing has been the same since he was called back to Greece after my excommunication."

"I know," he replied. "That must have been hard."

She finished her drink and poured another. "It was."

"Losing family like that." He shook his head. "A shame, that is."

Her thoughts drifted to her grandfather, and Gia froze, her face going pale.

Shadow lurched off the couch and went to steady her. "Sit down, Gia. What's wrong?"

"N-Nothing," she stammered.

"It don't look like nothing."

"I am fine. Honestly. Please, continue with the updates."

She listened to him as he rattled off his plans for stabilizing her cash flow. But she thought of the moment when her speargun pierced her grandfather, killing him. Inside her mind's eye, she could see his empty, dead eyes staring at her, and she felt like screaming.

39

June 5th

"I do not want you to go," Gia whispered to Florent. They were naked together under the sheets, her legs wrapped over his. She had barely let him out of her sight since he arrived in St. Moritz.

"I'll be back in three days," he promised her.

"I know, *amore*." She put her palm over his heart to feel it beating. "After everything that happened with Yiannis and Serena, I feel most secure when I am here like this with you."

"Mmm," he murmured lazily, "that sounds a bit like love to me, Gia."

The word made her feel sort of shaky and queasy, like an amateur tightrope walker, placing their toe onto the line, preparing to take their first step with no net below. The last thing she wanted was to let go and come crashing down with no soft place to land.

Florent felt her body tense up. "Shhh," he whispered. "It's all right. I won't make you say it again." For his part, Florent felt more secure as time passed. Forgiving Gia had broken open his heart, and no matter what happened, he knew that he would survive. Even if he lost her at this point, he felt he could finally move on. Of course, moving on wasn't what he wanted. On the contrary, he craved Gia as he always had. His desire for her had not waned, but his grip was less desperate, and he found great relief in letting go.

He placed his chin on the top of her head and breathed her in. Florent felt relaxed, but there was one thing that still rolled around in his mind, bothering him... something that created distance between them. A mystery he longed to solve. He wondered now if it might be the last barrier he would need to break before finally reaching her heart.

"I want to show you something, Gia."

He leaned over, opening the drawer in the bedside table. He pulled out his wallet and laid it on the table. He shuffled through the wallet until he found what he was looking for.

He passed Gia a folded note, stained with age.

She unfolded it and gasped. "This is written in my mother's handwriting! Where did you get this? What is it?"

"I was hoping you would tell me," he sighed.

She shot up, pulling the sheet around her. "What is this, Florent? Where did it come from?"

He took out the ancient gold coin from the wallet's change pocket and placed it in her palm. "This was found alongside the note at Suite 511 at the Hôtel Hermitage in Monte Carlo. Do you remember being at this place by chance?"

A soft cry escaped Gia's lungs even as she nodded her answer. It sounded like a strangled bird gasping its last breath.

"Have you seen them before?" he pressed.

Gia shook her head, no. She trembled.

Florent pushed on. "These items were found in a room your mother rented for *Adonis Papadonis*."

She shuddered and squeezed her eyes shut when she heard that name. It was all too familiar and the memories rushed back.

Florent kept his eyes trained on Gia. "Marina tried to kill Adonis in that suite, but he escaped."

Gia's pulse quickened, and she felt her blood rising under the skin below her ears. She finally found her voice. "No! That is not what happened."

"Then explain what actually happened. Because the last person who saw Adonis was your mother, and there is no denying the evidence... she attacked him in that room."

"Mamma was not like that... she... she was not *like me*."

"A murderer you mean?" Florent taunted Gia, hoping to unlock the door to the deepest part of her. There was no going back now.

Gia's eyes glazed over, and her mind took her back to that day in 1985. Gia was on the boat with her parents. They were leaving Monte Carlo a few days early, at her mother's request. The sun was shining. Everything was perfect... and then... it wasn't.

"Tell me, Gia," Florent insisted. "Tell me what happened."

"Mamma was... she was g–good," Gia stammered. "It was that horrible man's fault. He jumped onto our boat... and he—"

Gia dug her nails into her palm to keep from crying.

"It happened so fast," she continued. "He put his hands around Mamma's neck and tried to strangle her. She had to fight him. She... she was defending herself, you see. So she... she slit his throat, but—"

Gia couldn't stop the tears now. They rushed out of her just as they had the day that Marina died.

"Go on, *chérie*, tell me. Get it out. Let it go. Tell me everything."

Gia wailed, and it was hard for Florent to understand what she said next, but he got the gist of it. "Mamma hit her head when they fell... and they both died like that... so much blood. Red like the mouth of a demon. Blood everywhere."

Gia tucked her knees in, sobbing and rocking back and forth. In her mind, she wasn't really in the room with Florent anymore. She was in her daddy's arms, grieving her mother.

Florent wasn't finished with Gia yet. There was one last piece of the puzzle he needed. "And then? What happened next? Did you bury their bodies at Hotel Bauman like the others?"

However, Gia didn't even hear him. The sound of her tears and sobs were so loud that they drowned out everything else. She tried to gain control of herself, but could not.

40

June 7th

For Gia, the past two days had been some of the worst in recent memory. In fact, yesterday, she hadn't even gotten out of bed. The only reason for emerging from her cocoon today was because Riley was coming over.

Gia felt emotionally raw from all the crying. She didn't understand why Florent always probed into her past, pushing her to expose more and more of the secrets she had so carefully guarded. At last, he had emptied her troves. Was that what he wanted? Now he knew about everything.

Everything except Riley, of course.

No matter. Gia was going to take care of that loose end today and break things off with Riley.

Maybe Riley and I can play one last time before I send her on her way.

She smiled to herself and headed to the bedroom to change into something more revealing.

Security let Riley into Gia's suite.

"I am in the bedroom," Gia called out.

"Great," Riley shouted back. "Stay put. I'm coming in."

As Riley entered the bedroom, Gia let her long hair whish down from a topknot. She was wearing a full set of lingerie and a white silk slip dress.

Riley's eyes popped. "Jesus Christ, woman. I hope you know I am ripping that outfit off immediately."

"I was hoping you would," Gia said, giggling.

Riley looked sexy as hell, too. She wore drop-crotch jeans and a crop top. Gia stared at Riley's toned, tattoo-covered arms and fantasized about being held down by them and fucked hard.

Florent only had two modes when it came to sex: making sweet love or grudge fucking. Therefore, Gia felt slightly starved for rough sex and a good half an hour with her mouth between Riley's long legs. She was going to miss those long legs... and Riley's strong hands.

"Fuuuuuck, Gia," Riley whined. "You're making me wet just looking at you. Get on the bed. Let me see what's under that nightie."

Gia did as instructed, lifting the slip to show her hot pink lace underwear with a matching garter belt attached to silk stockings. She stretched out her leg and unfastened the first tie from the garter belt. "Take this off," Gia ordered, pointing at her stocking.

Riley tiptoed her fingers up Gia's leg to the loop and pushed it open. The stocking crumpled down Gia's thigh, and then Riley bit it, pulling it the rest of the way down her leg with her teeth. Gia bopped Riley's nose gently with her big toe.

Riley wiggled out of her crop top, exposing her small, round breasts and hard nipples. She climbed on top of Gia and used the stocking to tie her wrists together. Then she stuffed Gia's hands under a stack of pillows and whispered, "Don't move unless you want a spanking."

Riley took her time undoing the other stocking. First, she dragged her nipples over the silky fabric, feeling every thread caress her. Letting out a delighted moan, she finally freed the stocking. She stretched it out with both hands and snapped it like it was a belt. Then she wrapped it around Gia's mouth, tying it as a gag.

"Mmm mmm," Riley hummed. "You are a sight, Gia Acquaviva."

Riley then hopped off the bed and disappeared into the kitchen for a long time. A really long time.

Gia started to wonder what Riley was doing. She almost got up to go in search of her, but Riley showed up, holding a pair of scissors.

Riley dragged the point of the scissors all the way from Gia's foot to between the center of her legs. She snipped Gia's lace panties, exposing her.

Riley bit her lip. "Gia, I could slice you with these scissors if I wanted to, you know."

Gia furrowed her brow and shook her head.

Wooofpt, wooofpt, wooofpt... the scissors made sharp cuts into the silk nightie. Riley sliced the whole thing open and spread it apart. Gia's breasts sat plump inside the hot pink bra. Riley cupped them, kissing and licking them through the lace. After a few moments, she cut the bra open, too.

By this point, Gia was dripping. Riley slid several fingers in and Gia let out a muffled whimper.

"Do you want more?" Riley demanded.

Gia nodded.

Riley stretched two fingers open, making more room inside, and then slipped another finger in.

They locked eyes. Riley's mouth was open, and she ran her tongue across her teeth at the top, like a vampire might, before lurching for your neck. Riley used her knee to push her hand harder into Gia. Riley pressed the palm of her other hand down on Gia's clit to make pressure and in response, Gia pushed her hips up to meet Riley's touch.

They moved together like that until Gia climaxed, moaning into the silk stocking.

* * *

AN HOUR LATER, Gia was lying between Riley's legs. They were both spent. She kissed Riley's inner thigh.

"Riley, I need to tell you—"

"I'm so thirsty, Gia. I'm gonna grab some water. I saw some in the butler's pantry in the fridge back there."

"Those water bottles are for the security team."

"So? Can't I have some?"

"Bring some sparkling water from the big kitchen."

"But I want flat water."

"*Amore*, the guards drink that water and leave their food in that area. Leave it alone."

"Okay, fine." Riley slipped her pants on.

"Why are you getting dressed now?" Gia asked, feeling annoyed.

"Hello?" Riley snapped. "The guards? Not trying to show them my muff today."

"Be quick about it," Gia fussed.

Just as she had before, Riley took fucking forever in the kitchen.

Gia yelled, "Are you lost, *amore*?"

"Coming!" Riley answered.

She arrived with two glasses and a chilled bottle of Pellegrino.

Gia cut right to the chase. "Riley, I cannot see you anymore."

"Pardon?" Riley asked, nearly dropping her glass.

"I have to end things, Riley."

Riley scoffed and snickered. "Sorry, Gia, but your cum is barely dry on my hand." But then Riley locked eyes with Gia and it dawned on her that she wasn't joking. "Are you fucking serious?"

"I am."

"What the fuck! Jesus, Gia. Why did you seduce me, then?"

"I wanted us to remember our last time together."

Riley crossed her arms in front of her chest. "This is *not* our last time together."

"It must be."

"*Why?*"

Gia exhaled in exasperation. "Because it must."

Riley glared at Gia. "You're leaving me for that fucking useless *dude*? For real? No. Fuck Florent. I won't stand for this."

"Riley, do not make this harder than it has to be."

"Ha! Says the woman who just fucked my brains out. Nuh huh. No way, Gia. You don't want to leave me. I can *feel* it."

"What do you expect me to say?" Gia huffed. " You are right. I do not want to end things, but I have come to the point where I must choose between the both of you. And I want to make a relationship work with Florent."

Riley rolled her eyes, and venom entered her voice. "Sure, Gia. Okay. We'll see about that."

41

June 7th

Awa and Harper lounged by the pool at Langley Manor, sipping on fresh lemonade.

Harper sighed. "It's so much more pleasant to come to my parents' house with you living here, Queen."

"I'm grateful to be here, Harper. Thank you."

"How are things working out with Talia? Are you going to submit a book proposal soon?"

Awa grinned. "A book, yes, but much more than that. Steven Scotch wants to pitch a television show."

"Narrative or reality?"

"Just call me Queen Awa *Kardashian*."

"No!" Harper squealed. "You cannot be serious!"

"Harper, I desperately need funds. A few deals should help with that. I cannot live in your parents' mansion forever. I have to help my son rebuild in Senegal and get our people back home."

Harper sipped through her paper straw, lowering her sunglasses. "Well, I hope that you will consider OTN when pitching your show."

"Am I missing something?" Awa asked. "OTN is a news network, is it not?"

"We are branching out. I have a lot more latitude on the OTN mobile app."

Awa grimaced. "Please don't think I am being coy, Harper, but Steven Scotch is in conversation with HBO and Netflix... he sees the show as being prestige reality television."

"I see," Harper huffed. "Don't forget us little people when you're famous." Then she stuck out her tongue to let Awa know she was only kidding. "I respect your hustle. Really, I do. Now... you promised me a political scoop. I'm all ears."

"In Brazil last week, President Bowden more or less strong-armed all the Atargatic leaders into joining a Pentagon task force."

"Wow." Harper hopped off her chaise lounge and dipped her feet in the pool. "I can't say I'm shocked. The reaction to the Venice flood has been..." she winced and made a high-pitched sound, "Errr... *really, really* bad."

Awa nodded, chewing on her lip.

"So," Harper continued, leaning in closer, "what's the task force all about?"

"MWMD."

"What in the hell is that?"

"Magical Weapons of Mass Destruction," Awa explained.

"Oh, for fuck's sake." Harper rolled her eyes. "You know what this means, right?"

Awa dropped her head and smirked. "I have a fairly good idea, but I am interested in your take."

"The generals are going to get *just enough* information from all of you to form the basis for a legitimate war. Until now, the public has been very Pro-Mermaid. They're going to need to turn the people against you. *Don't let them.*"

"I'm not sure how I can stop it, Harper. The train is already in motion."

"Shit. This is very bad."

"I know," Awa groaned.

The wheels were spinning in Harper's mind. "Could you... if you had to... could you mount a defense?"

"Against whom? The U.S. Navy?" Awa balked.

Harper cringed. "I mean... yes."

"Harper," Awa dropped her voice to a whisper, "you cannot say things like that, darling. It's grounds for treason. What if they're..." Awa mouthed the next word, "listening?"

"Fuck you, U.S.A.!" she screamed at the top of her lungs. "Don't mess with my friend! Are you listening? I'm only kidding! I love all things Americana! I'm Harper fucking Langley after all! I'm Miss America!"

Awa buried her head in her hands and then said, "If you are indeed listening, this child really is joking!"

42

June 8th

"I have decided to leave my wife," Florent declared, taking a slow sip of whiskey from a crystal tumbler.

Gia slid open the door to the suite's balcony. She stepped outside and slipped off her robe, easing her naked body into the jacuzzi. "I do not know if I am ready for that step, Florent."

He admired her curves from a distance. He struggled to believe that after all this time, she still looked relatively the same. Then again, there was so much he didn't know about mermaids.

And now, Gia's emotional distance felt like a betrayal.

He knew that the conversation he had initiated about Adonis had been difficult for her. Digging up the past had sent her reeling, and he knew it. Even so, he wanted her to open up, and despite feeling much more confident over the weekend, he now felt insecurities creeping in. A large part of him wanted to hurl his heavy glass right at her pretty head and end the madness, once and for all.

He took a final swig and then snapped at Gia, going in for a verbal strike. "Maybe if you stopped spending so much time with that *actress* you might feel differently about my news."

Gia's heart flopped. She realized that she hadn't been careful enough with Riley, and she'd been caught.

Florent breezed out to the hot tub and ran his hand on top of the steaming bubbles. "I don't understand why you hide the truth from me, Gia." He sucked his cheeks in, trying to stop himself from saying anything else, but he had to let his feelings out. Even if Gia didn't care, he couldn't hold the poison in. "You are *mine*. You belong to me and to nobody else."

"Florent, I belong to no one."

"That is not what you have told me these last few months, Gia!" he screamed. "It's not what your body and your heart told mine only days ago!"

"Do not raise your voice to me." Gia reclined in the jacuzzi, dipping her hair in the water. Florent's jealousy always bothered her, but tonight she found him particularly grating. "If you want to go, then leave. Security can show you out."

"*Security can show me out?*" he snickered. "*Incroyable.* Did it not occur to you that Shadow might also have loyalty to *me*?"

Gia scanned his face. "Are you threatening me?"

He stood in silence, the muscles in his neck tensed. "Why are you acting this way toward me? I held you for hours while you cried."

"*Si*, Florent! I did! Because you *forced* me to reveal painful parts of my past that I put away long ago."

"I just want to be close to you, Gia. I swear. I wasn't trying to hurt you," he pleaded, new emotion in his voice.

Gia went on the offense. "But you *did* hurt me." She cut across the water, nearing him. "You cannot imagine how much pleasure I would take in slitting your throat right now."

"I don't have to imagine!" His face went a shade of violent red. "*Putain!* I nearly died less than two kilometers from this very spot!"

Florent's words sent a tingle down Gia's arms. He instantly discerned the thirsty look in her eyes.

"It is always murder with you! You never think of anything else!" He stomped inside and yanked the sliding door closed with a thud so loud that Gia thought it might fall out of its rut and come crashing down.

Gia settled back into the water, grateful for a break from him. She knew that later on she could placate him with their torrid little sex games. Maybe if he humiliated her and smacked her ass, he would calm down. That seemed to be the default reset anytime she bruised his ego.

He has to learn, Gia thought. *I do not need him to rescue me or poke around inside my head. If things are to work between us, he must let me be myself.*

She let her tail unfurl as she floated on top of the jacuzzi's water. Flicking a spray of water over the railing, Gia watched it cascade out into the night sky.

"Quit that," a voice whispered. "You're getting me all wet."

Gia sat straight up. "Riley?" She swam over to the edge of the hot tub and peeked out over the ledge, to see her lover hanging from the beam of the room below.

Riley flashed a smile at Gia. "Hey there, Killer."

"*Merda!*" Gia fussed. "What in the world are you doing out here?"

"Practicing my parkour."

"Unbelievable." Gia massaged her temples and sunk deeper into the jacuzzi. "What wonderful security I have. Are you planning to hang upside down like a bat all night?" Gia whispered to Riley.

After a few moments, Riley made her way up and over the railing, landing like a cat behind the jacuzzi.

"Florent is here," Gia said in a low tone. "You have to leave *this instant*."

Riley's eyes sparkled. "I know Florent is here, Gia. That's why *I'm* here."

Gia's eyes widened with fear as Riley's intent dawned on her. "No, you cannot mean that."

"Tonight's the night," Riley replied, leaning against the wall of the hot tub. "I'm ready."

Before Gia could get out a word, Florent flung open the patio door. The suction squealed as it peeled apart.

"I can't do this anymore, Gia," Florent yelled. "Something has to ch—"

But at that very second, Riley leapt out from behind the jacuzzi and stormed her way over to Florent. She reached into her sleeve and pulled out a sharp serrated knife.

Gia froze in the water, unable to move.

Florent ran backwards, trying to escape Riley without turning away from her.

"*Sécurité!*" he shouted.

Riley lurched towards Florent, bringing the knife closer to his neck.

"Riley!" Gia screamed. "Stop this!"

Florent flailed as he grasped for Riley's arms, trying to knock the knife out of her hands.

Riley bobbed and swayed, evading his grip.

Gia felt powerless, as if she were in a vacuum someone had unplugged from the wall. Something about the way Riley and Florent were sparring felt familiar. She was swept into a wave of sense memory. She was no longer watching Riley and Florent. Instead, she saw her mother and Adonis, and her horror was so intense that her vision blurred.

Riley lunged at Florent again, and this time the tip of the knife grazed his Adam's apple. He kept the knife from shoving into his neck by wrapping his hands around Riley's arms and pushing them away.

"Help me, Gia!" Florent yelled to her. "Where are the guards?"

Riley grinned. "They're not coming, Florent. I drugged their water yesterday."

"Help! *Aidez-moi!*"

Gia sat motionless in the jacuzzi, seized by a sense of terror so great that she could not move.

Florent kicked Riley in the stomach, and she hunched over for a second, giving him the time he needed to wrestle the knife away from her.

He backhanded Riley with the knife, slicing into her neck, cutting her from end to end.

Her wound opened like the mouth of a child's toy.

Blood spilled out onto the deck in a waterfall.

Riley grabbed her throat, trying in vain to stop the bleeding.

Realizing what he had done, Florent felt glued in place. Watching Riley bleed out in front of him transported him twenty-five years into the past. He experienced that familiar trauma reflex and grabbed his own throat. He could feel all the pain Riley was experiencing.

He dropped the knife.

Riley tried to reach for it, but he kicked it across the patio.

He turned his attention to Gia, who was still in the water, dumbstruck. She was in a daze, seemingly catatonic. He screamed, "Did you two plan this together?!"

However, taking his eyes off of Riley for just that moment gave her time to attack him again. Before Florent even noticed, Riley was running toward him with all the speed she could muster. She ducked her head like a ram and used her body weight to tackle him. Instead, the impact propelled them both toward the railing. Their bodies crashed into the barrier and skidded over the edge.

Gia pierced the air with an otherworldly wail.

Riley and Florent careened down, down, down—locked together in a deadly embrace.

Their bodies landed with a muted thud—and it was Pierre's face, yet another image from the past, that settled into Gia's mind.

Gia hoisted herself up to peer over the edge. She spotted her two lovers many meters below, broken on the jagged cliffs. Their lifeless bodies looked like discarded rag dolls.

For a moment, she was sure they would stand up, and Riley would explain that it was all an elaborate prank. But Gia knew that wasn't true.

Her skin went cold as she felt a sharp pain in her chest, as if a clumsy giant had accidentally stepped on her heart and smashed it into pieces.

43

June 8th

Gia's heart thumped in her chest as she ran through the hotel suite. She dressed as quickly as she could and went to Serena's room to retrieve her. The baby was sleeping and screamed when Gia picked her up.

She opened the door to the adjoining suite, where the guards stayed when they were not on duty. She wasn't sure how long the guards would be knocked out. Gia wasn't even sure if they would wake up at all. God knows what Riley drugged them with.

Gia plugged up Serena's mouth with a pacifier and listened at the door to the hallway. She could hear commotion and shouting outside.

Suddenly, there was banging on the door in her suite.

The hotel manager and several concerned guests had gathered outside her door.

"Miss Acquaviva, please open the door!" the manager yelled.

"Use your key!" someone shouted.

She heard the electronic click of the door to her suite, and the manager and the nosy guests immediately hustled in. At that exact moment, Gia took Serena and fled out of the guards' suite, bursting down the hall and into the stairwell. She bolted down the stairs and out a side door into the forest.

Having spent so much time in St. Moritz over the years, both with Serge Dupont and on her own, Gia knew the trails well. She ran as fast as she could, and when she finally got a safe distance away, she called Shadow.

"Come immediately," she panted into the burner phone, out of breath. "Florent is dead! The police will be at the hotel soon!"

"Where are you?" Shadow asked.

"I will be in the lake by the hotel."

"You can't stay there. They'll be looking for you."

"*Merda!*" She bounced Serena in her arms to keep her quiet as she tried to think of something else.

"Gia, listen to me," Shadow spoke intentionally slowly to calm Gia down. "I'm looking at the map now. There is a creek in the north-west part of the lake that runs through the mountains. It'll take you out of town. There's a recycling center a little more than ten kilometers north of St. Moritz. I'll have a team meet you there tonight. Be careful and godspeed."

When she hung up the phone, Gia heard police sirens in the distance. She dashed toward the lake and dove in, holding Serena in her arms.

* * *

Gia hid in the cab of a bulldozer with Serena. Thankfully, the baby was fast asleep, exhausted from sprinting through the stream with her mother. Sometime in the middle of the night—Gia wasn't sure what time because she had neither a watch nor a phone—Shadow's men came for her. They hid her in a soundproof compartment in the bottom of a small work van. Once mother and child were secure, they locked everything up and drove deep into the mountains, toward the Italian border.

Roughly two hours later, Gia and Shadow's hard men arrived in

Lake Como. They rolled past the gate to a palatial villa and through manicured gardens into a garage. Once the garage door closed, they unlocked the van's compartment and helped Gia and Serena climb out.

"*Madonna!*" *La Nonna* stood at the van's tailgate, tapping her foot. "Waking an old lady up in the middle of the night is madness! I swear, one day you will give me a heart attack, *Signorina Acquaviva!*"

For once, Gia was thrilled to see her fixer, and she threw her arms around the old woman.

"Come on," *La Nonna* said, patting Gia's back. "Come inside and I will cook you some pasta. You must be hungry enough to chew your tail off."

* * *

Gɪᴀ ᴛᴡɪʀʟᴇᴅ fresh tagliatelle around her fork and slurped it up. The sauce was creamy with mushrooms and salted butter, absolutely delectable. *La Nonna* poured Gia a glass of crisp white wine, and Gia guzzled it down.

"You are a good cook, Donatella," Gia noted, between mouthfuls.

"Ah... my grandchildren are very picky eaters, but they all like pasta. I have a few decent recipes."

"Where are we?" Gia asked.

"Much to my daughter's dismay," *La Nonna* sighed, "we are at her house in Lago di Como. She does not like it when I bring my work home with me, so I am making a special exception for you... my favorite client."

Gia smirked. "You must say that to all of your clients."

La Nonna winked. "More wine?" She topped off Gia's glass and then invited her upstairs, to the guest room. "*Signor* Shadow will be here in the morning. Finish up your wine and get some rest."

44

June 9th

"Breaking news," Harper said to her ever-growing OTN audience, "last night in the luxury ski resort town of St. Moritz, Switzerland, a Hollywood star, Riley Rose was found dead, along with the body of French shipping magnate, Florent Bisset. Details are still emerging in this shocking case, but I can confirm *exclusively* that the crime scene includes... sorry folks... this is shocking for me. All things considered, it really should not be so shocking to me... the crime scene encompasses the hotel suite of my niece's mother, the world's most famous mermaid, Gia Acquaviva."

Harper let the revelation land before she continued.

"We're going live to our local affiliate in St. Moritz."

The producers cut to a Swiss newsperson, holding a microphone, posted outside Gia's former hotel. "This is Château Gelé," the reporter said, "the most exclusive hotel in St. Moritz. It is a veritable playground for the rich and famous. But last night, it was the scene of a gruesome crime. I have a woman here with me who witnessed some of the action."

The newscaster thrust a microphone toward a woman with puffed-up lips and enormous diamond jewelry. "*Madame*, what can you tell us about what happened here last night?"

She answered in a thick Russian accent, "I hear lot of screaming. A man making lot of noise, scream 'Help!'. So I call hotel lobby and tell them I hear fight or something. I go out to balcony to look, to see what happening, you know. And when I go to balcony, I see most horrible thing. Two people falling in sky... down to rocks. Very dead."

The newsperson's mouth had dropped. "Very dead indeed. And, *Madame*, did you see Gia Acquaviva? Did she have anything to do with these alleged murders?"

"Gia Acquaviva? Mermaid?"

"Yes, the *billionaire* mermaid who has been plagued by rumors and murder suspicions for years."

"I see no mermaid. Only see very dead movie star and man."

The newscaster nodded. "Back to you, Harper."

The producers flipped back to the studio in New York. Harper had a serious expression. "We are actively investigating this case and will report details as they develop. Trust me, you will want to stay tuned to OTN. We will have insider information that you can't get anywhere else."

* * *

GIA WOKE WITH A SPLITTING HEADACHE. When she couldn't sleep the night before, she'd snuck back down to the kitchen in *La Nonna's* daughter's house and finished the entire bottle of wine. She felt lousy.

Thankfully, *La Nonna's* daughter had taken Serena early that morning and fed her a good breakfast. Serena was finally eating baby food, so there was no need for the seamilk nonsense anymore.

Gia finally stumbled downstairs to find Shadow playing on the floor of the living room with Serena.

"Oof," Shadow remarked, "looks like you had a long tumble down the kitchen sink."

"What?" Gia snapped.

"Bit hungover, are you?"

Gia did not reply, but instead went in search of coffee and did not return until she had a cup in her hands.

La Nonna was on the sofa, giggling and making slurpy sounds at Serena.

Gia crumpled herself up into an armchair. She had been so shocked and terrified yesterday that she had had no time to process her grief. The truth of what had happened crashed around inside her like a wrecking ball, tearing everything down. She wanted to go to sleep and never wake up again.

Watching *La Nonna* and Shadow behave in such a carefree and nonchalant manner only made her feel more depressed.

I should have stopped them, she thought. *I could have stopped Riley if only I had tried. Florent is dead because of me. Why did I not get up and help? What is wrong with me? I ruin everything good in my life. I destroy everyone. Vittore is right. I run from love. I destroy everything. Maybe I deserve to be in jail. Certainly everyone would be safer if I were locked away.*

Shadow noticed that Gia was lost in a daze. He left Serena with *La Nonna* and sat down next to Gia.

"You all right?" he asked. He shook his head and sucked his teeth. "Of course you ain't. Come 'ere."

He wrapped his arms around Gia. He was big, like a tree, and she leaned into him, wanting to cry and being unable to. She only trembled.

"Shhh..." he whispered. "Shhh. It's all right. Everything will be all right. I know you didn't hurt them. It wasn't your fault, Gia."

She relaxed into his grip and stayed there for quite some time. Apart from Vittore, she had barely allowed herself to be comforted by anyone. Her vulnerability with Florent had been recent and hard-won. But with Shadow, things felt easy. Maybe it was their shared mermaid ancestry or the fact that they were both career criminals of a sort... she wasn't sure, but Shadow felt safe to her.

She collected herself and then said, "We have a lot to discuss."

La Nonna was ready, and so was Shadow.

Gia began. "If it has not happened already, it will happen soon... there is going to be an explosion of information about me... about my... my *crimes.*"

Shadow and *La Nonna* said nothing just yet. They listened.

"Florent had been following me for years," Gia explained. "He knew almost everything about the murders... the identities of the bodies removed from under the Hotel Bauman. He threatened me and said that if anything ever happened to him, that he had left instructions to release a file of evidence to the media. I imagine that is coming soon."

"What kind of evidence?" *La Nonna* asked.

"I do not know. Florent never said."

La Nonna nodded. "I will reach out to my contacts and see if I can get a copy of his file."

"Also," Gia continued, "there is the matter of the loan from Bisset Industries."

La Nonna winced. "The acceleration clause."

"Yes," Gia replied. "Shadow, we have to halt re-opening the casino in Macao. In fact, I think I will need to liquidate my holdings there and in Sydney, Australia. The palazzo and casino in Venice are both destroyed. I still do not know if insurance will cover the cost. We will need to sell—"

It was very difficult for her to get the next part out, because it hurt her.

"We have to sell my jet. That will cover the bulk of the debt to Bisset Industries."

Shadow bobbed his head. "Understood."

"The more I think of it," Gia said, slipping into a kind of daze, "the more I think that maybe it would be best to sell everything and focus only on my casino in Monte Carlo. I can live on my yacht there and slowly rebuild my portfolio. Sometimes I wonder if I overextended myself by expanding into South America and Asia Pacific."

Shadow reached out for her hand, taking it in his. "Gia, now it's better to focus on one thing at a time. Don't try to solve all your problems in one day. Me and Miss *Nonna* are here to help you. Let us worry about some of that, all right?"

La Nonna walked over, carrying Serena. "Believe me, I have dealt with worse crises in my life."

Gia narrowed her eyes. "That does not seem possible."

La Nonna scoffed. "Do I need to remind you that I represented *Signor* Quintilio Mosca for many years? Believe me. I have shoveled manure much more pungent than this."

45

June 10th

"Good evening, everyone, and welcome to tonight's show." Although Harper had a juicy hour ahead, she felt stiff and anxious. She had tried so hard to nail Gia in the past, and now she had all the evidence of Gia's crimes in her hands. But Harper did not feel triumphant; she felt sad.

Why? Was it because she had grown so close to Awa and had a newfound appreciation for mermaids? Was it because she knew that Gia going to jail would leave her niece with no parents? Or had Harper become so hardened about murder after offing Royce and Bronwyn that she felt any killing could be justified?

Whatever the source of her confusing feelings, she had to lock them away for the time being and deliver an hour of infotainment to the masses.

"Early this morning, a trove of evidence was sent to OTN and to media networks all over the world with proof of Gia Acquaviva's crimes. The Gia Acquaviva File came with a signed letter from Florent Bisset. The letter is dated approximately one year ago. I will read it to you now."

Harper cleared her throat and then began, "My name is Florent Bisset. I met Gia Acquaviva when I was eighteen years old. She was beautiful and cunning, and I fell deeply in love with her. At the time, she was dating my father. He gave her everything he had, and I believe she meant to kill him, but he died in an accident. Gia is a cold-blooded killer. In fact, she tried to kill me by cutting my throat, as she did to so many others, but I lived. After what happened to me, my life's mission became discovering her secrets and exposing her. If you are reading this letter, it is because Gia has murdered me."

Harper paused for a moment, letting the information land. She blew air out of her cheeks and then said, "Wow. That is heartbreaking stuff."

Behind her, on the green screen, images of documents appeared. "The file contains evidence of a dozen or so murders committed over a twenty-five-year period, including the murder of Spanish movie star, Nicolás Ángel Fernández."

"If you remember, several years ago, security footage was leaked showing Gia with Nico in his apartment building. There was also a sex tape. But nothing conclusively linked Gia to his murder, and the case was dismissed by the Italian court."

"The file shows flight records, GPS data, detailed reports on Gia's movements, photos, video, financial records... in all my years working as a journalist, I have never seen anything so comprehensive. It's clear that Florent Bisset was intent on showing the world just how truly evil Gia is."

"My brother lost his life after becoming involved with Gia... although not by her hand. We still don't know the reason why mob boss Quintilio Mosca killed Cameron, but perhaps it was a feud that he got caught in the middle of... whatever it was, my brother paid the ultimate price after falling in love with Gia."

The camera pushed in on Harper for a closeup. "Gia is a very dangerous woman, and right now, she's on the run. We want to call on you to help us find her. Visit StopGia.com for more information."

46

June 15th

Queen Mother Awa and Prince Moussa shuffled through the sunlit atrium inside the Pentagon, escorted by an underling of the U.S. Secretary of Defense. They arrived in a meeting room draped with American flags, as well as flags of the Air Force, Army, Marine Corps, and Navy. Into the room paraded a line of generals and administrators. The purpose of the meeting was two-fold: first, it was a show of force, an intimidation tactic, and second, Pentagon officials were tripping all over themselves to participate in the task force meetings. So instead of causing a staff uprising, the Secretary of Defense let all the high-ranking members attend.

In truth, it was Defense Secretary Glover and General Thomas, the head of the Joint Chiefs of Staff, who ran the show.

Glover introduced himself first, shaking Awa's hand. "Your Majesty, thank you for coming. And Your Majesty, King Moussa, we have been looking forward to this. Please, let's sit."

The key players took their places. The rest of the generals and officials hung around the edges of the room in a circle that was two or three people deep.

"So," Glover began, "this is the Chairman of the Joint Chiefs of Staff, General Thomas. He will be your key pointman for the task force."

General Thomas nodded his hello.

"Take it away, General," Glover said, relinquishing the floor.

"My pleasure," Thomas replied. "Project Blue Whale is a top priority for us at the moment. We hope that it will be a unifying venture for the Mermaid and Human worlds."

"Pardon me," King Moussa interrupted. "We prefer to be called the Atargatic nations. It is more inclusive language."

Thomas and Glover exchanged a glance that indicated they were either amused or irritated. Moussa couldn't tell.

"Understood, Sir," Thomas acquiesced. "The United States' position on this possible alliance between the Atargatic and Human nations is that it could prove fruitful for all parties. It could bring peace, food stability, and possibly even a radical shift in Climate Change. We are eager to understand more about Magical Weapons of Mass Destruction and their impact on world conflict. Nuclear weapons have maintained peace on a global scale, but with Russia and China shifting their military strategy, the Pentagon is highly motivated to investigate the use of natural warfare. Make no mistake, we do not condone the attacks made by the Atargatic nations, but we are... interested."

Awa folded her hands, laying them on the table. "Let's first turn our attention to your use of the term Magical Weapons of Mass Destruction. We object to classifying Elemental Magic in this way. Instead, going forward, we prefer to use less conflict-ridden terminology and simply call it Magic. Could we agree on that?"

General Thomas looked to Secretary Glover for his approval. Glover nodded.

"We are amenable to that," the General replied. "But we would like a better understanding of... Magic."

Awa smiled. "We are aware. It's why we are all here, is it not? King Moussa, please take the floor."

"*Alors*," Moussa said, reaching into his briefcase to pull out several sets of handouts, "we have prepared a deck for you outlining the three kinds of Magic accessible to merfolk: Sea Magic, Ice Magic, and Sky Magic."

"Is there such a thing as Fire Magic?" the General asked.

Moussa shrugged. "General Thomas, *fire* has always been an obsession of humankind. And while fire is destructive, *water* is much more powerful."

The message landed as intended, and the room filled with whispers for a moment.

"Turn to page four, please," Moussa directed. "Here you will find an abbreviated history of our Magic to read in your own time. Instead of presenting everything to you, we thought we would give you time to ask us whatever you like."

The General summoned one of his direct reports, who passed him a clipboard with a checklist. "I would like to go through this if you don't mind. Please answer with 'yes', 'no', or 'unsure'."

Moussa and Awa agreed.

"Do you have control of the ocean's creatures? In other words, can you command them at will?"

Moussa wasn't sure. Awa answered, "Unsure."

The General ticked a box, "All right. Can Ice Magic be used to reverse the effects of global warming?"

Moussa replied, "Unsure."

"Can Sky Magic be used for necromancy, specifically resurrection?"

Moussa sighed, "Yes."

"Can Sky Magic be used to control the movement of the sun and moon?"

"Unsure."

"Could Sea Magic be harnessed as a form of renewable or non-renewable energy?"

"Mmm," Moussa pondered the question and then thought about

all the ways the Greeks had used Sea Magic to power their colony. "Yes."

"Interesting," the General noted.

The inquisition went on for another twenty minutes or so. Finally, Secretary Glover and General Thomas rose and shook Awa and Moussa's hands.

The General's eyes were dancing with delight. "This has been very enlightening."

"Gentlemen," Awa concluded, "we hope that this meeting shows you our interest in continuing to build a strong relationship between our nations."

47

June 20th

Gia had been hiding out in Lake Como for ten days, unable to step outside the walls of *La Nonna's* daughter's villa, for fear of being spotted. She had no choice but to stay inside and watch her world fall down around her.

Shadow and *La Nonna* were doing their best to control the collateral damage, but Florent's file had lit the media and the public on fire.

That morning, Shadow and *La Nonna* sat Gia down at the kitchen table. Shadow grimaced and began, "I have some bad news, Gia. The Italian authorities have seized your jet."

"*Merda!* You could not sell it in time?"

"*Bene, allora,*" *La Nonna* explained, "we sold it, but because the prosecutor has filed charges against you, the government invalidated the transaction and clawed it back."

"Is there anything we can do? Can you file an injunction or something?"

La Nonna shook her head, no.

"There's more," Shadow continued. "There's been protests at all your properties. Widespread outrage. The doors to every establishment have been closed, as of the start of business today."

"No!" Gia screamed. "They cannot do this!"

La Nonna sat down next to her client. "Unfortunately, Gia, they are well within their rights. We need to talk about options for Serena."

"What do you mean... *options*?" Gia cried.

La Nonna glanced at Shadow and winced, hoping he would tell her the next bit.

He took the old woman's cue. "Love, you ain't got a lot of choices at this point. We can hide you for... I don't know... a year... maybe? But sooner or later, the bottle and stopper... they're gonna get you."

"Speak proper English, please!" Gia snapped.

Shadow exhaled sharply. "The bottle and stopper... the coppers. The cops! The police! They're not going to stop comin' for you. I been thinking, Gia... we could go to London. I think my family would take you in. We been hiding unseen in the River Thames forever. No one would ever find you there."

Gia dropped her head in her hands. "Shadow, let me ask you something. Could you live your whole life underwater, knowing that London was just above your head but out of reach?"

He frowned.

"I will take that as a no."

La Nonna slammed her hand on the table. "We will fight this!"

"How?" Gia whispered.

"I have been thinking," *La Nonna* explained, "that there may be a persuasive legal argument to be made that you are not, in fact, a human being. As such, you are not a *person* as defined by statutory law."

Gia perked up. "Explain what you mean."

"If you are not a *person*, then you could not possibly have committed crimes, if the laws are to be read strictly."

"Could that work?" Shadow asked.

La Nonna threw up her hands. "I am a damn good lawyer, so I will do my best!"

"That sounds like a good plan," Shadow replied, trying to sound encouraging. "And the coppers, can you keep them away from here for a while longer?"

La Nonna snorted with laughter. "The police would not dare to come here. I am still on the mafia payroll, remember?"

Gia bit her lip. "Donatella, what happens next?"

"As I said, you must decide what happens to Serena. Who will take custody? Harper is the natural choice. She is family."

"No! Harper will exploit Serena if she thinks it will help her get ratings." Gia thought back to the battle in Venice—to Shadow and how he had kept Serena safe. "Shadow, could you take her?"

He sucked his teeth, "Love, I wish I could, truly. But I got a record. No court would grant me custody of a baby."

"It must be Vittore then," Gia decided. "He is the only other person I trust. Draw up the paperwork."

"I will do that now," *La Nonna* replied.

48

June 25th

Deep below the Osaka Bay in Japan, the Archivist, Togashi, paced the spiral hallways of the Great Library, searching for an ancient text that had been misplaced. The shelves contained more than one hundred million books and scrolls, so if meticulous organization was not maintained, important items could easily get lost or go missing.

The loudspeaker chimed, and then Akiko's voice boomed in the speakers. "Togashi, please come to the vestry."

Togashi hopped into a golf cart and drove a mile deeper into the Great Library to meet Akiko.

She bowed. "Ah, here you are! We've been waiting for you."

Queen Karen snooped around a locked cabinet, smudging the glass with her fingerprints, which very much annoyed Togashi. Karen whipped around, and the beaded fringe on her leather cape hit Akiko in the face.

"Ouch," Akiko said, rubbing her cheek.

Queen Karen appeared to be agitated. "Togashi, I've been waiting for five days in my tiny guest quarters to see you. I don't understand why the rooms are so small here. Where have you been?"

"My apologies, Your Majesty, but I have been engaged in complicated research. I am translating several ancient scrolls and texts to uncover more about Sky Magic."

"Mmm hmm," Karen whistled through her front teeth. "See, the thing is, I don't enjoy wasting time. I understand you like poking your nose into dusty books... it's your passion or whatever... but instead of spending your energy on theoretical pursuits, why not help me get ahold of Serena Acquaviva? Doesn't it make more sense to finish what we started so that you can study her, rather than trying to make sense of fading words on a page, scribbled thousands of years ago?"

Togashi nodded. "I will concede that there is merit in practical study as well as theoretical, yes."

"Fucking intellectuals," Karen muttered under her breath. "I'm not sure if you're aware, Togashi, but there's a manhunt underway for Gia. And, when the police find her, that will give us an opportunity to swoop in and steal the kid. I think we should make a game plan."

"As you wish, Ma'am."

Karen stuck out her lips and puckered her face. "So, what? Does that mean you're going to help me?"

"Why would you need my help?"

"Are you serious?" Karen spat. "After Venice, I'm a bit low on resources. I need some troops and I need transportation. Let's not forget that I've been the one taking the heat for your errands, Togashi."

"True," Togashi agreed.

"You're really frustrating me right now. I don't want you standing there nodding like a bobblehead doll, I want you to strategize with me. Let's figure out how to get our hands on that baby."

49

June 28th

G eneral Thomas arranged for a military seaplane to fly Queen Mother Awa to the Arctic Circle. Skirlor was waiting for her at the meeting point. Awa left the Americans behind and set off with Skirlor on her diplomatic mission. They walked for a long while across the tundra, until they came upon an electric vehicle hidden under a camouflage tarp. They boarded it, and Skirlor swept them across the thawing landscape to the vast, virgin waters of the Arctic Ocean.

They entered the ice shelf through a secret passage, and Skirlor gave Awa a special wetsuit that would keep her warm until they reached the Glass Castle, the home of the Ice Folk.

They strapped themselves to a power board that ferried them deep into the ocean to the hydrothermal vent around which the colony was constructed. Black smoke billowed in cloudy puffs from the magma chimneys along the seafloor. Red and white tube worms feasted on the mineral-rich emissions. A cast of snow white crabs scuttled past, in search of a resting spot and a good meal.

They arrived at the Glass Castle, a tall and sprawling structure made of pieces of obsidian which had been welded together over centuries. The palace reminded Awa of the work of Gaudí, because the walls featured undulating ridges and intricate mosaics. Skirlor showed Awa to her quarters and let her rest after the long journey.

* * *

LATER THAT EVENING, the Ice Folk performed traditional music and dancing for Awa. Rows and rows of children swayed to the sounds of sea flutes and shell drums. Awa played her part and smiled, but in reality, she found their instruments to be irritating. Their music reminded her of meditation tunes streamed through speakers in luxury spas. Nothing disturbed Awa's relaxation more than a fucking pan flute.

Afterward, over cups of Arctic Sea Moss wine, a local delicacy Awa did not care for but nonetheless endured, she spoke with the Ice Folk Elders about her involvement with Project Blue Whale.

Skirlor translated from their ancient language into Atargatis for Awa.

"Why are you helping the Americans?" the Elders asked.

"The United States demands cooperation with the threat of violence."

"A bond formed with resentment creates knots in the soul," they said.

Awa sighed. "I fear the animated corpse that is America is devoid of a soul."

The Elders chattered away, their tinkling voices like the sound of falling icicles. "The World of Man seeks no true cooperation, only domination."

"Yet in the world today," Awa rightly noted, "Man is the ruler."

"The tides are rising, Child of the Sea. We will reclaim the surface once again."

* * *

WHEN THE OFFICIAL GATHERING CONCLUDED, Skirlor took Awa to another wing of the palace.

"Queen Mother Awa, we are preparing for the battle to come."

Inside a massive gymnasium, Ice Folk trained in the ancient magical arts. Spell casters fashioned strange weapons from ice. Others recited incantations of invisibility. Others constructed tools of warfare.

Awa asked Skirlor a final question that she knew was all in vain. "Is there no chance the Ice Folk will join the alliance with the humans?"

Skirlor looked deep into Awa's eyes. "Why should we help those who seek to destroy us?"

50

June 30th

Gia sat in front of the computer screen, waiting to connect with Vittore. Her heart was beating fast. To her right and left were Shadow and *La Nonna*. They had only left her side the past three weeks to carry out business on behalf of her and their other clients.

When Gia saw Vittore's face pop up, smiling, she began to cry. "*Methusalamme*," she whimpered, "it is so good to see you. I wish you were here."

"So do I, *tesoro mio*." He reached out and put his hand near the camera, as if stroking her hair. "Stavros and I have canceled the wedding."

"This is why I am calling you, *Methusalamme*, I want the wedding to go forward as planned."

"No!" he screamed. "Not without my Gia. *Assolutamente no!*"

"Listen to me, old man," Gia said between sobs. "I will be there."

"Do not be ridiculous, Gia. You cannot take a chance like that. Remember Venice? No more chances. Are you listening to your advisors?"

"*Signor* Cantalupi," *La Nonna* replied, "this is actually my idea."

"You cannot be serious!" he yelped. "My wedding is not a focus for now! No! Gia's safety is the priority. The only priority! Do you hear me?" Then he cursed under his breath.

"*Signor* Cantalupi," *La Nonna* continued, "I have been negotiating with the Italian authorities. They have agreed to allow Gia to attend your wedding in Greece under my watch, and then we will immediately return to Italy, where she will turn herself into the authorities."

Vittore wept, and his lips trembled. "What do you expect me to say, ah? Wonderful plan? No! This is terrible news. This is a terrible idea, and I will not do this."

"You *will* do this, *Methusalamme!*" Gia insisted. "This is what I want, all right? And you and Stavros will take care of Serena until I can secure my freedom. I am begging you. Your happiness is what I want, and I want to know that you... at least... have the family you always wanted. I have to face what I have done. And I believe that doing it this way... seeing you marry someone you love... this will give me the strength I need to hold my head high and walk toward the challenges I will face."

Vittore turned away from the camera. His shoulders shook, and Gia could hear his muffled cries. He wiped away his tears and turned around. "As you wish, *tesoro mio*. I will not fight you anymore if this is what you really want."

"It is," she replied firmly. "I will see you in two days in Santorini. Shadow has arranged for security, and I am sending a party planner to help you get Uncle Stavros's hotel ready for the wedding."

"I love you, *tesoro mio*," he said. "All I want is to hold you close to me."

"I want that, too, *Methusalamme*."

Gia burst out into tears.

51

July 2nd

There was not a cloud in the sky on the morning that Gia, Shadow, and *La Nonna* arrived in Santorini. Gia no longer had her jet, but that did not mean she was going to slum it in a commercial flight quite yet. *La Nonna* arranged with a mafia client to fly Gia to Athens, and then Shadow paid for a helicopter to Santorini.

Someone in the Italian police had tipped off the media about Gia's deal to turn herself in after Greece, and so when the chopper landed, the runway was buzzing with paparazzi. Shadow already had a team of guards there to help with crowd control.

Uncle Stavros had closed his hotel to tourists, so only his children and grandchildren were there. Vittore loved being around Stavros's big family. They all doted on the sweet old man, and they were thrilled that their patriarch had found love again in his golden years.

Apart from all the chaos happening around Gia, which made Vittore sick with worry, his life was lovely. In fact, he had often wondered lately if the mess with Gia was God's way of evening things out, because how could anyone be allowed to be as happy as he was with Stavros?

Vittore heard the commotion outside the front of the hotel as Gia arrived. Shadow and his hard men got Gia through the front door, and she rushed immediately to Vittore. They embraced each other and cried.

* * *

STAVROS SET up a late breakfast for everyone by the pool, while the grandkids took turns playing with Serena. The catering company and the florists arrived to set things up for the wedding that evening. Stavros handed Gia a frappe, and she thanked him.

"How can you drink this disgusting thing?" Vittore asked, plugging up his nose.

"Ah, *Methusalamme*, do you not remember Mamma drinking frappe? She loved it! She used to make one for me every afternoon after school."

"Horrible," Vittore replied. "I have to bribe the grandchildren to make me espresso."

"It is so good to see you, *Methusalamme*. I have missed you so much."

"As have I, *tesoro mio*." He pulled her closer to him and dropped his voice to a whisper. "I need to speak to you. *Alone*."

They moved to an empty part of the patio and sat down in chairs across from each other.

"Gia, tell me the truth... did you kill Florent?"

She dropped her mouth. "How could you ask me that? Of course not! I loved Florent."

"*How could I ask you?*" he balked. "Have you seen the news, *tesoro mio*? I am an old man, but I read the paper! How could you do all those things, Gia? It shocked me to hear about all of it. I could not sleep for days. Murder! Why do you do that to people?"

The color washed out of her face, and she went numb. "I...I..." she could not find the words to explain to him what drove her intense desire for violence.

Finally, Vittore filled the heavy air with his words. "What happened to you as a girl should not have happened. Your father and I should have dealt with the bodies... not made you hide them down in that cave. I cannot imagine how hard it must have been to see your beautiful mother die the way she did. But *tesoro mio*... what you have done..." He turned away from her and stared out at the sea for a long time.

Gia sighed and closed her eyes. "Vittore, I wish that I could tell you I am sorry. That I regret doing all I have done. I do not. I am not sorry. I enjoyed it, and I would do everything all over again if I could. I would do it better than I did. I would probably kill more people, if you want to know the truth. I know that I am sick... that something is wrong with me. People should not behave as I do."

She opened her eyes to find tears running down his cheeks. It hurt her so much to see him crying.

"You are not who I thought you were, Gia."

His words stabbed her right in the heart.

"I am sorry I make you feel this way," she whispered.

"Me?! I am the last person you should feel sorry for. What about the family and friends of all those people you killed? When I helped you with Nico... when I suggested you meet *La Nonna*, I did this because I thought... I do not know what I thought... I suppose I thought you hurt him by accident. How stupid of me."

Gia crawled onto her knees and put her head in his lap. "Forgive me, *Methusalamme*. I cannot bear it if you do not love me anymore."

"Forgive you, Gia? It is not for me to forgive you. That is for our Father in the Sky to do. Understand?" Then he raised his hand and held her cheek in his palm. "Of course I love you. There is nothing you can ever do that will make me stop loving you. I do not understand you. I am mortified and sickened by all that you have done. It will haunt me until my last days, but, child, I love you more than you can ever imagine, and I always will."

She buried her face in his lap, and her hot tears fell on his legs. "Thank you, thank you. I love you. I love you so much."

He stroked her hair until she calmed down.

When she looked up at him again, he asked, "What will you do, Gia?"

"The only thing I can do, *Methusalamme*. I will fight."

* * *

AFTER A NAP, Gia woke up feeling a bit better. It was her last full day of freedom, so she had to milk it for all it was worth.

Gia walked up behind Vittore and gave him a bear hug. "Off with you," she commanded, releasing him. "Time for you to meet the tailor and put the final touches on your suit."

He scurried away, and she marched out to the patio to check on the progress of the wedding decorations. They were not elaborate enough.

"More flowers, please," Gia ordered.

The florists had already erected lattices over most of the buildings at her uncle's hotel, but since the whole terrace had to be covered by fabric to block paparazzi from taking photos, Gia wanted everything inside the tent to be as lush as possible.

She inspected a cardboard box filled with fresh-cut roses and hydrangeas, approving them. Fairy lights were strung inside the tent, making everything glow. Wedding magic was underway.

She checked her Rolex and saw that she was short on time, so she scampered inside to get dressed. She smiled into the mirror, applying a bold shade of pink lipstick, which made her think of Talia. She said a silent thanks to the universe for being rid of the PR woman.

I never imagined I would find such pleasure in dressing myself. I do not miss Talia's army of stylists. I should enjoy putting on makeup and beautiful clothes. Soon I will wear a prison uniform. Who knows if I will ever feel silk on my skin again?

Uncle Stavros popped into her room, holding Serena, bobbing

her in the air. "And then," he said in a baby voice, "the big claws will drag you down, down, down to Cold Currents."

Gia turned and tisked at her uncle. "Stop that! You will scare her, Uncle!"

"Do not be a spoilsport, Gia. The baby does not understand me. Let me enjoy my great-great-grandniece."

Rolling her eyes, Gia couldn't help but smile at her uncle's antics. "Where is the ring?" she asked.

Panic flashed across her uncle's face. "Oh, no! The ring!"

"Father in the Sky!" Vittore yelled, hobbling into Gia's suite. "You are both very lucky that *someone* on this little island still has a good memory. I have *both* rings. Here." He placed the two boxes on Gia's vanity and draped himself over the foot of Gia's bed. "Now," he huffed, "bring me my grandchild."

Stavros motored her over, making jet engine noises with his lips. "A special delivery for my young lover." He put baby Serena on the bed next to Vittore.

"No-no!" Serena babbled.

"*Nonno? Nonno?!* Gia! She is saying *nonno!*"

"*Methusalamme,*" Gia replied, "I do not wish to break your heart, but her favorite word right now is 'No'. I believe she learned it from her grandparents in New York."

"Nonsense! You heard her just as I did. She is saying hello to her *nonno*. And I will say hello back to her, with a kiss." He pushed her shiny blonde hair off her forehead and planted one on her. She responded by puckering her lips and blowing some spit out.

Vittore giggled. Stavros took his hand.

"My young lover," he said, "are you ready to become my husband?"

Vittore's eyes went soft. "Today, and for all the days I have left. Although I cannot imagine there will be many."

"Do not count on that!" Stavros scolded him. "You have your sky god, and I have my water goddess. For all you know, I may cast a love spell on you. And if I have done that... then maybe I can cast a spell to make you live forever!"

Vittore winked. "I would settle for twenty more years."

"The two of you almost make me believe in love!" Gia sighed.

Down the hall, someone called out for Stavros, "*Bampa!*" It was one of Stavros's sons. He ran into the room, breathless. "The police are here."

"Police?!" Vittore screeched.

"They say that they are here to arrest Gia," Stavros's son explained.

Gia's eyes blazed over to Vittore. She shot up and bolted to the window, throwing it open. However, her suite faced the pool, not the ocean.

And there was no way to dive into the water and escape this time.

La Nonna rushed into the room before the police could.

"What is going on?!" Gia howled. "They are not supposed to take me now! The deal was for Italy... for tomorrow. I was supposed to be allowed to have today, tonight with Vittore. You must stop them."

La Nonna paced the room. "The Greeks must want the news coverage for being the big boys who caught the world's most famous mermaid. I am so sorry, Gia. There is nothing I can do for you right now. You must go peacefully into their custody."

Gia threw herself onto the bed next to Vittore and embraced him, pulling Serena in close to her as well.

"*Methusalamme*, please," she begged, "promise me that you will take care of Serena and keep her safe."

"You know that I will!" he sobbed.

The police chief came to the door and *La Nonna* introduced herself to him. He waited a moment more for Gia to say her goodbyes.

"Come now, Gia," *La Nonna* said softly, "the police are ready."

As she left the room, Shadow's face hung in a frown, but he said, "We will see ya real soon, love. Chin up."

52

July 2nd

The Greek police strip-searched Gia and threw her in solitary confinement. A team of guards questioned her, probing her about every aspect of her life and about whether she could do Magic. They had all seen the footage of the attack on Venice, and they feared a similar fate might befall them. Ultimately, they decided it was safest to leave Gia strapped to her bed.

That night, as she sweated in her tiny, hot cell all by herself, she wondered for the first time if the murders had really been worth the price of her freedom.

53

July 6th

"Welcome back, OTN viewers. I'm Harper Langley, and I am coming to you live from outside a small prison facility near Athens, Greece. Gia Acquaviva has been inside this building since her arrest four days ago. This is a story that has rocked the world with its shocking details of alleged cold-blooded murder. In a moment, Gia's attorney, Donatella Sapienti will hold a press conference, and then I will be joined by the world's second-most-famous mermaid... my personal favorite mermaid, might I add... Queen Mother Awa Diop of Senegal."

* * *

BRIGHT LIGHTS BURNED down on *La Nonna* as she sauntered to the podium set up in the parking lot of the Greek jail where Gia was being held.

La Nonna ran her fingers through her short grey hair and then stood up straight, projecting total confidence into the camera.

"Good evening, I am Donatella Sapienti, and I represent Gia

Acquaviva. I would first like to say that the Greek authorities have *not* allowed me to consult with my client since her arrival here four days ago. This directly violates both Greek laws and European agreements. I will file the appropriate claims to rectify this situation. Second, I would like to address a few items that have been reported falsely in the press. My client did not murder Florent Bisset or Riley Rose. There is a mountain of evidence that will prove her innocence. However, as to the other murders... I am aware of the abundance of so-called evidence that Mr. Bisset released to the media. My team and I are combing through it. Understand that *not all evidence* will ever make it into *any* court in *any* country. We cannot litigate important matters on twenty-four-hour news coverage. What I will say regarding my client's defense is that laws are made by men for men. My client is not a human being, so, as a first step, we will file for a dismissal."

The crowd began whispering, and the whisper became louder and louder until everyone was shouting.

The angry energy scared *La Nonna*. She closed the press conference by saying, "I will not take any questions." A team comprising Shadow's hard men and her own mafiosos whisked her away.

* * *

HARPER'S SHOW returned from commercial break. "Unbelievable," Harper growled into the camera. "I'm almost at a loss as to where to begin. Whew. Wow. What a press conference. Every time I think I have a handle on where this case is going to go, I get thrown for a loop."

The camera zoomed out, making room in the frame for Awa.

"Your Majesty," Harper began, "how did that land with you? Specifically, what did you think of Donatella Sapienti's words 'not a human being'?"

"Thank you for having me once again, Harper. I first want to say that I am friends with Gia... I don't think that is a surprise for your viewers, but I do feel that it is an important fact to disclose. Regarding your question... Donatella is right, in technical terms, Gia and I are not human. We are not primates. Mankind is descended from apes. Mermaids are not. We are amphibians."

Harper gave Awa a sideways glance. "Mmmm, I don't know about that, Queen Mother Awa. If you're quote-unquote not a human being, does that mean you never have to be accountable to any laws? Seems unfair."

"Lawmakers make laws, Harper. I'm not a politician, remember? I am a queen."

"Are you at all concerned that an argument like the one Donatella is trying to make might backfire? In other words, what if someone were to say to you... oh, I don't know... you don't deserve human rights because you're not a human being?"

"Harper, there is a difference between being biologically human and having humanity."

"Mmm, I love that, Queen Mother Awa. Someone print *that* on a t-shirt!"

54

July 6th

Akiko passed Queen Karen a pair of long-range binoculars. Per Togashi's instructions, Akiko had engaged a helicopter pilot to fly the both of them over Stavros's hotel in Santorini to search for Serena.

"Dammit," Karen cursed. "The hotel is all boarded up. Where in the hell have they taken that fucking baby?"

"I don't know," Akiko replied. "But sooner or later, we will find her."

55

July 12th

"Are you well?" Awa asked Gia. The women were on two sides of a thick glass barrier in the jail outside of Athens. Gia was overjoyed to see a friendly face after days in isolation. "How were you able to come to me?"

"Friends in high places," Awa replied. She then silently mouthed the words, "The FBI sent me."

Gia flashed a worried look. "Queen Mother Awa, this time I think I may have gotten into a bind I cannot escape."

"I'm not so sure about that, Gia. You have caused a revolution, certainly within the Atargatic world, but also in the World of Man. You disrupted the balance, you see. No one has captured the imagination of the people like you have. There is much power in persuasion, as you well know."

Awa approached the barrier and whispered to Gia in Atargatis through the small holes in the glass, "Child of the Sea, Spawn of Clay, you carry within you the spirit of the two worlds. You can change *everything* if you play the game as you should."

Gia tried to take in everything Awa said, but she had many questions. There was so much Gia didn't know, so much she failed to understand.

Awa returned her thoughts to the recruitment mission she had been given, knowing full well that she never intended to carry out the orders of the Pentagon. She was firmly on Gia's side and always would be.

She leaned forward with a knowing smirk. "Gia, Uncle Sam wants you."

56

EPILOGUE

East of Crete, in the deepest part of the Mediterranean, the riptide curled its icy fingers around Queen Zale.

Zale the Ancient had communed with the Gracious Tides in Cold Currents these past many months. The shivering whispers had shared many secrets of old with the silver-haired queen. She was plump with knowledge and eager to do the bidding of her gods.

She had but one desire: to break open Serena and unleash the full force of the power contained inside the child.

A many-eyed beast, the Gracious Tides could view any place in the world through a single droplet of water. There was no hiding for little Serena. The Gracious Tides knew exactly where the child was being kept, and they murmured to Queen Zale that the time had come to collect the girl.

IF YOU LOVED THIS...

Love this book? Leave a review!

Dying to know what's next for Gia?
Pre-order the next book in the series today!

WANT MORE FROM ME RIGHT NOW?
Simply scan the QR code below and join my Insider Circle.

SCAN ME

ALSO BY JINCEY LUMPKIN

Mermaid of Venice (Book 1)

Mermaid of Sicily (Book 2)

Mermaid of New York (Book 3)

Mermaid of Paris (Book 4)

Mermaid of St. Moritz (Book 5)

Mermaid of Monte Carlo (Book 6, coming August 2022)

Sirena de Venecia (*Mermaid of Venice*, the Spanish language version)

Made in the USA
Columbia, SC
01 August 2022

64404760R00111